THE HAJAR BOOK
OF RAGE

elements: I

Edited by
Farhaana Arefin

 Hajar Press

Contents

Editor's Note   *vii*

Playlist   *xi*

Untitled
Rasheed Rollins

I

two stones
Aria Danaparamita   3

The Preliminary Flame Before a Kiss
Yasmin Alrabiei   5

An Exercise in Neutrality
Laetitia Keok   II

Musarrath
Nafeesa H.   13

Sequence from a Dream
Jiaqi Kang   15

American Sonnet, After Terrence Hayes
Malika McKenney   35

Diss Track Sonnet
Christian Yeo Xuan   37

In the Absence, Fire
Malak Hijazi   39

thinking about rape in the courtyard of a coffeeshop
Bidhya Limbu   45

Application for Social Housing in Tower Hamlets
Mymona Bibi   47

Broken Parrot: Warrior Tongue
Simran Kaur Johal   49

October for Another Century
Nur Turkmani   67

the damage has been done
Mandy Shunnarah   69

Mites
Aurora Leode Fadonougbo   71

Labour Day, May 1
Nicole Morris   77

atlanta ii
Banah el Ghadbanah   79

The Fireflies
Sarah F. Abdullahi   81

The Blacksmith II
Gospel Chinedu   89

A Country That Carries Its Dead Like Firewood
Oladosu Michael Emerald   91

About the Authors   *93*

THE HAJAR BOOK
OF RAGE

EDITOR'S NOTE

Our decision to launch the *elements* anthology series with *Rage* was unanimous. I don't know if it's because I'm a Fire sign, said one person during the editorial meeting, but I think anger is the starting point for political action—it's how I know what needs to change.

Anger is instructive, we wrote in the call for submissions for this book, *teaching us what we're fighting against and what we're fighting for.* As someone whose own anger has always felt too volatile, dangerous and untrustworthy to admit to, I found this narrative neat and redemptive. Anger could be useful, ethical, righteous, drawing battlelines between right and wrong, prefiguring care in the midst of brutality. When I stand with you in love and rage, I am saying, *I do not abide this injustice and I will do anything for our liberation.*

Anger is the fuel of direct action, protest, revolution. In the inflation of fury, we are unassailable agents of history, so ready for liberation that we already feel free. *No justice, no peace! When do we want it? Now! The people united will never be defeated! I believe that we will win!*

Why, then, do I struggle with anger? Something about it flickers not only with political potential but also with terrible political risk. I come back to the initial question: what, and whom, are we fighting? Revolutionary rage points its incandescent finger at the man-made, death-of-man-making structures draining us and the earth of life.

We are angry with the architects and functionaries of the racial capitalist order, we are angry with the powerful, we are angry with the system, the state, the superstructure, the cruel, complex, anonymous machinery of organised abandonment and violence, we are angry with God. In this we are one movement, our struggles connected, our rage shared—*the people united*. Yet the flame of anger flickers, unruly and uncontrolled. In a moment's time, you will hurt me, or I will hurt you, and what then? I stand *with* you in love and rage. Can I also stand against you?

You must be angry, my friend said when I answered the phone. I'm fucking furious, I said. I'm sorry we let you down so badly, they said. Do you know what hurts the most, I said. Everything that I believed in and that all the people I love say they believe in, this whole thing we say we're doing and building with each other, that when the world crushes and kills us *we keep each other safe*—it's all just a fucking lie.

What do we do with anger that has nowhere to go? What do we do when *what we are fighting against* is each other?

Anger is instructive, and it is also vicious and awful. It brings violence and the threat of violence, saying, *I want to hurt you back*. I hold my anger in, afraid of torching my loved ones when I burn down the world.

The day after Claudia died, my windscreen was smashed. I drove home alone in the dead of night, stricken by awe and fear of the football-sized spiderweb decorating the thick glass as ominous proof of the fragility of the boundary between myself and the world. In the dark, I parked outside my building and sat in my car for an hour, screaming and sobbing with uncontainable rage.

Claudia was full of rage. Last summer, we went to a discussion led by a queer abolitionist organiser about race and resistance in the UK. Between a relentless timeline of modern-day anti-racist uprisings against state-sanctioned murder and a string of crowing anecdotes about direct actions that had led to the arrests of the speaker's friends, the audience was ordered over and again to *get organised, join the movement*. At the end of the talk, in something of a daze, I turned to Claudia and raised my eyebrows. Well, that was rousing, I said perfunctorily. I didn't think so, Claudia frowned, actually, they started to really piss me off.

In an instant, I became aware that my own body was in a state of activation. I wasn't inspired—I was pissed off too. Why had we all been pummelled with a list of the most grievous brutalities and collective traumas our generation had lived through, without warning or care? Why were we being bullied into taking part in forms of struggle that would endanger our safety and expose us to state violence, whatever our vulnerabilities might be? And why was caring for each other—all the work of social reproduction, performed disproportionately by racialised women, which keeps communities alive—being excluded from this narrative of anti-racist resistance? Racism isn't just riot police, Claudia said, I would have received better cancer treatment if I were a white woman, and that's racism too. I nodded, wondering why I hadn't known anything was wrong, why I hadn't felt my own anger without her.

For thousands of years, Indigenous communities the world over have used fire to tend to the natural landscape. Traditional knowledges developed over generations of interdependent living with the forest teach that fire clears away dead organic matter, fertilising and aerating the soil, encouraging new growth.

As part of the colonial project of land expropriation, forced displacement and cultural genocide, European settlers in Australia and the Americas criminalised Indigenous burning practices. Fire was a risk and needed to be forbidden, eliminated. In fact, these smaller fires had prevented larger, hotter, more devastating ones, regularly consuming the dry undergrowth and deadwood accumulating like fuel on the forest floor. I think of the tinder building up between us all, waiting for a spark.

The winter before last, I saw how rage regenerates. In the crowds on Whitehall, Claudia voiced anger at an old friend, gripping her *HERBALISTS FOR A FREE PALESTINE* banner stiffly like a spear. Away from the battlefield, my sister and I held her. You didn't deserve it, I told her. I didn't, she said. The protesters marched on. Later, in the cinders of confrontation, Claudia and her friend walked arm in arm under her banner, forged back together by the fire.

Weeks later, when I felt like ash, incinerated by my own anger at my betrayal, Claudia pulled me close and didn't let go.

A month after Claudia died, I watched my sister plant flowers in a bed of flaming tulips, so big and bright they looked fake.

Claudia hated the phrase *we keep each other safe*, she said, her fingers caked in soil, her eyes aglow under the baking sun. Because we don't. We need to do better.

This collection is for my friend Claudia Manchanda.

To clear the ground for something better.

To give our rage somewhere to go.

—London, July 2025

PLAYLIST

Max Roach – 'Absolutions'
Chosen by Rasheed Rollins

Dara Puspita – 'Surabaya'
Chosen by Aria Danaparamita

Curtis Mayfield – 'Pusherman'
Chosen by Yasmin Alrabiei

Mavis Staples – 'We Shall Not Be Moved'
Chosen by Laetitia Keok

Naseebo Lal & Akram Rahi – 'Kachchi Pencil'
Chosen by Nafeesa H.

The Strokes – 'Ode to the Mets'
Chosen by Jiaqi Kang

Mitski – 'Buffalo Replaced'
Chosen by Malika McKenney

Saint Levant feat. MC Abdul – 'Deira'
Chosen by Christian Yeo Xuan

Julia Boutros – 'Thoouar Al Ardh – ثوار الأرض'
Chosen by Malak Hijazi

Gil Scott-Heron – 'The Revolution Will Not Be Televised'
Chosen by Bidhya Limbu

Pan Sonic – 'Urania'
Chosen by Mymona Bibi

Sampha – 'Blood On Me'
Chosen by Simran Kaur Johal

Bedouin Burger, Zeid Hamdan & Lynn Adib – 'Ya Man Hawa'
Chosen by Nur Turkmani

MASTER BOOT RECORD – 'BIOS'
Chosen by Mandy Shunnarah

Abdullah Ibrahim – 'Mindiff'
Chosen by Aurora Leode Fadonougbo

Tiken Jah Fakoly – 'Plus rien ne m'étonne (Live Salle Pleyel)'
Chosen by Nicole Morris

Nxdia – 'OUCH'
Chosen by Banah el Ghadbanah

Ed Sheeran – 'I See Fire'
Chosen by Sarah F. Abdullahi

Chase Noseworthy – 'Blacksmith, Blacksmith'
Chosen by Gospel Chinedu

Burna Boy feat. Chris Martin – 'Monsters You Made'
Chosen by Oladosu Michael Emerald

UNTITLED

Rasheed Rollins

Song: Max Roach – 'Absolutions'

An urgency wrapped, packaged
in sheets of doubt

                                        conveyed to you

through
commerce and you want to shout—
No.
Howl,
       let

            out
a shriek or two,
all forlorn

                                  at the present.
Having such purpose within your grasp,
                        it still

      somehow

                                    eludes
                         you.
But you swear—

You swear.
You have something,

                    TREMBLING
               within your clenched fist.

TWO STONES

Aria Danaparamita

Song: Dara Puspita – 'Surabaya'

strike
she says
and sparks of flint
shall spur forth
fiery rage
that engulfs
all

two stones
clandestine
we the colonised
pocket between folds of skin
like contraband cigarette
lit through the window
slit

in this prison
fingernails scrape
maggot rice from the floor
when afar, gunfire
we have lost the smell of
blood in the thunderclap of
cordite

we wait
promise we get out
gunpowder and grenade
no more bamboo
spears we will
set the bengawan
alight

let them
see surabaya
blaze in sea of fire
strike, she says
and trust in god
in time our rage
will engulf

all

THE PRELIMINARY FLAME BEFORE A KISS

Yasmin Alrabiei

Song: Curtis Mayfield – 'Pusherman'

Kissing, much like fire, is a primal force. It flickers with the potential to warm, to consume, to leave traces of heat long after the kiss itself has extinguished. Consider the kiss as a chaotic ballet of proximity, a vector of longing where unspoken truths converge. If you've ever hovered at the edge of a kiss, you'll know it's not the lips that matter—it's the space before them. That taut suspension and the breath held too long. A kiss holds the power to excite and the persuasiveness to make sure we surrender ourselves entirely. It encourages a dynamic filled in equal parts with tenderness and urgency. As Iranian poet Forugh Farrokhzad writes, 'A kiss lit a flame between lips,' illuminating the kiss's dual role: the initiation of warmth, but also, a flashpoint of untamed possibility.[1]

There exists a moment before the kiss. A charged interstice where desire has not yet materialised, but is no longer dormant. That liminal heat, the cusp of touch, is what I call the preliminary flame. With the power to completely reorganise time, this flicker of heat is what makes a body remember it's alive. Fire itself doesn't start with contact;

---

[1]   Forugh Farrokhzad, 'The Kiss', *The American Poetry Review*, Vol. 35, No. 1, January/February 2006, https://aprweb.org/poems/the-kiss, accessed 5 June 2025.

it starts with tension. It is not passion fulfilled, but the conditions that allow passion to combust. A threshold. In phenomenological terms, it is the anticipation that constructs the event. In political terms, it is the ignition point for something irreducibly volatile.

There is a through-line with the element of fire. It doesn't only destroy. Fire is also transformation. And the political context of any fire starts with the systems built to prevent it. Who is protected when the flames rise? The first organised fire brigade—the Vigiles Urbani of Ancient Rome—weren't just civic heroes. They were enforcers of imperial order. When the Great Fire of 64 AD devoured two-thirds of the city, rumours spread that Emperor Nero had lit the blaze himself. Reconstruction was an opportunity for imperial expansion. Fire, then, becomes a question not only of heat, but of narrative. Who lit it, who benefits, who is blamed?

My first encounter with *The Kiss* by Gustav Klimt was not in a museum or a textbook on Viennese Symbolism, but on a war-torn wall in Syria. Tammam Azzam's photo-montage, which transposes Klimt's gilded lovers onto the facade of a bombed-out building in Damascus, seizes the painting's original Art Nouveau context and reanimates it as political critique.[2]

It becomes a palimpsest—love inscribed atop ruin. As an Iraqi whose cultural context of identity was heavily informed by my childhood trips to Syria, I immediately wanted to know more. I showed everyone. It was one of the first posts I shared to Instagram, back when I made an account in 2015.

In its original form, *The Kiss* speaks to historic anxieties

2   Tammam Azzam, 'A Kiss is Just a Kiss', Atassi Foundation, n.d., https://www.atassifoundation.com/features/a-kiss-is-just-a-kiss, accessed 27 May 2025.

about the boundaries between sensuality and sublimation. The lovers are rested in a golden void, at once grounded and abstracted. Klimt renders the male figure in rectilinear patterns, the female in circular motifs, coding gender differences in aesthetic terms. Their fusion is both erotic and dangerous; the kiss appears consensual, but the man's hands grip her face and body with a near-total possession. It is a lover's act gone obsessive.

When Azzam remediates this image onto Syrian rubble, the context totally collapses. Created in the aftermath of Azzam's exile from Syria in 2011, *Freedom Graffiti* becomes a layered response reconfiguring both Klimt's romantic sublime and the architecture of devastation it now inhabits. Its rapid spread across digital platforms culminated in its inclusion in Banksy's Dismaland. Azzam's work does not aestheticise ruin. It insists that beauty, far from being extinguished by catastrophe, persists as a mode of endurance, a counter-archive, a way of insisting on life when so much conspires to erase it.

Beyond Klimt's painting I have a second favourite image—a kiss that similarly unsettles the binaries of tenderness and terror. In the footage of a prisoner exchange in Gaza, an Israeli hostage, Omer Shem-Tov, kisses the heads of two Hamas fighters before returning to Israeli custody.[3] Most headlines framed it as 'SHOCKING', unable to reconcile the image with their binary scripts. Commentators reached for easy diagnoses—Stockholm Syndrome, psychological collapse, manipulation. But the image pulsed with something far more unruly and ambiguous, defiantly

3   'Israeli captive kisses head of Hamas fighter during prisoner swap', Al Mayadeen English, 22 February 2025, https://english.almayadeen.net/news/politics/israeli-captive-kisses-head-of-hamas-fighter-during-prisoner, accessed 27 May 2025.

refusing to be decoded. What if a kiss isn't meant to be understood, only felt? Is the kiss the last act that we have that is truly ungovernable?

We've been conditioned to expect a rigid protocol around hostage exchanges in the context of Israel and Palestine. Names tallied like commodities, numbers calculated, terms brokered through intermediaries like Egypt or Qatar. These are moments choreographed by the logic of the state: transactional and sanitised. The kiss detonated that choreography. It ruptured the military script, veered violently off course. No language prepared us for this utterly human gesture.

In this case, the kiss didn't just subvert expectations. That flashpoint of intimacy became offensive, destabilising binaries of captor and captive, good and evil, power and powerlessness. The kiss exposed the fault lines in our geopolitical narratives, inviting us to look again.

And that's precisely the point. Kissing transcends language; it is an embodied gesture that resists singular meaning. It can be loud or hushed, private or public, spontaneous or ceremonial. We kiss lovers and children, icons and corpses, the hands of elders and the lips of strangers. Some kisses are inherited through ritual of greeting, others born in moments of rupture. Yet kissing is not a universal freedom. It is deeply political. Who is allowed to kiss? Where? How big is the expanse between the kiss in the nightclub and the kiss in the cathedral?

Western media all but ignored the moment. Its departure from the carefully staged theatre of recent decades' propaganda rendered it illegible, unusable. But among Palestinians and much of the Arab world, the kiss resonated as both proof and provocation. Proof that resistance could be humane. Provocation against the narrative monopoly of Western moralism.

8

This is not a gesture that can be understood outside of the overlapping, colliding histories of Zionist occupation, Palestinian resistance and the structural asymmetries of global power. Both Azzam's montage and Shem-Tov's kiss dislocate the kiss from its romantic safehouse. They return it to its material conditions. Some kisses are of love, some are of play, some even of rage. And rage, as Audre Lorde reminds us, is not destruction for its own sake. In her 1981 keynote presentation at the National Women's Studies Association Conference, Lorde said, 'my anger and your attendant fears are spotlights that can be used for growth.'[4] Rage is information. It is clarity. It is a fire that reveals the architecture of what must be undone.

The preliminary flame—that anticipatory heat before a kiss—is where both desire and defiance live. It is the moment before contact where the body decides whether to touch or to turn away. In both the Syrian wall and the Gaza exchange, the flame leaps. The kiss is given. And in so doing, it redefines the terrain of what information a kiss can carry.

What ties Klimt's *Kiss* to the viral image of Israeli hostage Omer Shem-Tov kissing the heads of his captors is not merely the shared gesture, but the way both images break the fourth wall of their contexts. They reveal how gestures of care, when staged within systems of violence, carry the power to unsettle, to short-circuit the entire spectacle. Like Klimt's lovers on a crumbling wall, Shem-Tov's kiss exists as both beauty and provocation. It incinerated the billion-dollar question, 'do you condemn Hamas?' *I kiss Hamas.*

---

4   Audre Lorde, 'The Uses of Anger: Women Responding to Racism' (1981), *Sister Outsider: Essays & Speeches by Audre Lorde*, Berkeley, CA: Crossing Press, 1984, p. 124.

The kiss is often cast as tenderness incarnate—personal, private, soft. If you have ever been in love, you'll know that a kiss can set you on fire... but only some kisses set the world on fire. When tenderness becomes tactic, and passion turns to strategy, the whole planet gets butterflies in its stomach. I'm talking about kisses that expose the fracture between closeness and control. Kisses that melt. Kisses that burn.

AN EXERCISE IN NEUTRALITY

Laetitia Keok

Song: Mavis Staples – 'We Shall Not Be Moved'

Fill in each blank with a suitable word.   (15 marks)

We walk, (1)___*neutral*___, to the bus stop. We take the (2)___*neutral*___ bus to the (3)___*neutral*___ train station. On the train, a disembodied voice over the intercom says, (4)___*neutrally*___, 'Please stand clear of the closing doors.' A boy puts his hand through the doors as they close. Why did you do that. Still, (5)___*neutral*___, we hold hands and wait out the disruption. The (6)___*neutral*___ disembodied voice now apologises for the delay, 'We apologise for any inconvenience.' His or mine. Mine or yours. Ours. The train stays in the station for ten more (7)___*neutral*___ minutes. The boy plays with his (8)___*neutral*___ uniform. He is now late for school where they will teach (9)___*neutrally*___ about genocide. That's okay, he will get an excuse slip for it. His teacher will excuse him (10)___*neutrally*___. He will sit at his (11)___*neutral*___ desk and learn the steps to self-preservation: Begin (12)___*neutrally*___. Move with (13)___*neutral*___ omission. Arrive always at harmony—the word, more than what it looks like.

What does it look like? Let's be precise. It's in our training. When, on our essays, our teachers wrote, be specific, they really meant: (14)___*risk nothing*___. Say the root of neutral is (15)___*neuter*___, to render incapable of generation. He was only trying to make it to class. *I cannot reconcile it.*

MUSARRATH

Nafeesa H.

Song: Naseebo Lal *&* Akram Rahi – 'Kachchi Pencil'

Heathrow, 1975

Waiting for my new husband in the crowd
Looking for his prized pointed Eidi ki topi *photo seh*
Oof so much noise, I can't smell his musk yet
Chwaarah, *calls my name,* Musarrath Musarrath
Is it you? Meh ao? Meh ao? *My* kuseh, *his trail*
Jakhni, dhaal, kurry-pakoreh *could defrost London*
For us—nah jee, Engrizi *people not greeting me*
He heard me call and later he tells me he'd thought
I'm cat meowing—meh ao? meh ao? *Funny man*
Shukar Allah mikki *funny man* laba—*you'd cry*
Because no way I would understand engrizi *joke*
He could make me laugh big not making me small
They stare, I think is Christmas not me they looking for
I thought I heard his voice calling me, Musarrath Mus—
Not him, I carry walking like Amma's smile, *to* acha gorah *officer*

Heathrow, 1979

Go, go akhna Junnah, ohs mikki *back room* vich fir karya
Junnah mikki akhna—*remove your* clothes
Meh sharmindha oi giyahn—*woman doctor, please?*
Akhiyahn-neh moor lay tha, akhna: *no. Now don't be shy*
Quickly. Meh sochniya—ka patha

Mikki *no* **arrest** *no please, arrest* na kari shoran
Fir akhna mikki, saareh kapreh la—*remove all* clothes
Meh dari giyahn—maara junna kaptha kudhar? *No English*
Husband. Please, *no deport*
Akhna mikki: *calm down* ya meh thohki *restrain* karsahn
I'm bride, nah, *restrain* mikki kohni paha
Bateh neh hath, *cold, stop* meh *calm* meh *calm*
Kutha gadha, mikki chohr mikki chohr
Let go go go

my friend arrived in 1979 to be married, immigration man-doctor investigated her for virginity, 19—her shaadi in july, kuri kutha pregnant? nai! never touch any na-mahram, they don't believe her, yes they do this, they think she just wants free ticket, easy before she met her new husband, it was the law of then—open legs, prove it—she didn't tell me then, only now, meh dog-officer's legs arms panni throri mince him, bury. bad times, them times. welcome inglend, thoba oh veleh long gone. jisla engriz changi si.

SEQUENCE FROM A DREAM

Jiaqi Kang

Song: The Strokes – 'Ode to the Mets'

Will came to my house for dinner one time. When I told him to take off his shoes and he replied with, Yeah, I know, ethnic households, my mum is German, I burst out laughing. He didn't get it. I took his jacket, soaked all the way through, and he gave me a cold and clammy hug, his clothes sticking to mine. I was twenty-five. He was nineteen. His name on Signal was Kindling, like for a fire. I always thought of it like Kinder, children, Liebling, dear. That time we got arrested together, I could hear him singing in his cell, 'Bella Ciao' and 'Which Side Are You On?' and 'Solidarity Forever', or mainly just the parts of those songs that consisted of their titles. He sounded crazy. Like a werewolf, I imagined his howling face cast in wiggly square moonlight by the thick glass window set high up in the wall and pointing to the sky. Will, a friend of mine. We met at a protest. I helped him get down from a pole. He was just a kid. I loved him like a little brother. I would give him everything he needed, as long as he was willing to walk to me through the storm. But when he left, as I should've known he would, nothing I said could make him come back.

It had been raining all day, there must have been deep puddles all along the road. The wind was throwing the branches of the neighbour's cherry tree against the upstairs windowpanes, lacerations of rainwater against the glass. I worried something would shatter that the landlady would charge me for. I was already paying so much for gas, I had to blast the heating to keep away the mould. For Will I made pasta puttanesca, simple and sour, but with the scene outside I wondered if he'd show up at all. Then the doorbell rang and Will was there. He didn't have an umbrella, obviously. How easy it was to lure a kid like Will across the threshold: free food, cheap wine, the promise of conversation.

In my living room, Will pulled tissues from the box on my dining table to pat his hair dry while I finished stirring the sauce. His dirty and soggy keffiyeh draped across the radiator. He told me that he had spent the afternoon sending angry, bitter, firm, strongly worded emails. Nobody would ever read them, but someone still had to send them. What? I said from the kitchen. The emails still have to be sent, he hollered back. Right, I said. I turned off the tap, clattered bowls onto the table. His shit-eating grin. He passed me the crumpled-up handful of his tissues, I said thanks and put them in the compost. He was long and thin like spaghetti, it had taken four police officers to carry his body into the van because they'd been worried about dropping the middle of him. He inhaled his food in three mouthfuls and I realised I should've made more. While he waited for me to finish pushing my sauce around with my fork, he picked up the papers and books I had lying around on the other half of the table and examined everything carefully.

He flipped through the Wisam Rafeedie with the red cover that almost all of us owned, and I asked him if he'd read June Jordan. On one of the Post-it notes, I'd copied just a few hours earlier: *At dawn the student gave me a caramel / candy and pigs and dogs ran into the streets / as the sky began the gradual / wide burn and towards the top / of a new mountain 1 saw / the teen-age shadows of two sentries / armed with automatics / checking the horizon / for slow stars.* He'd like that one. It was written in Nicaragua with the Sandinistas, cows in the moonlight, the woman in the red shoes, so beautiful, had he heard of her? He asked me if I'd ever been to Nicaragua, 1 said no, he said me neither but I'd love to one day, 1 said me too but 1 don't know when or how, and he said yeah. 1 drank water. 1 said 1 remembered 1 had lent my June Jordan anthology to C. and he said he was seeing her soon because they were planning something new together and he could get it from her. The edition had left out 'Intifada Incantation: poem #8 for b.b.L.', which was suspicious, wasn't it? Will said he knew that one, it was stuck to the bedroom wall of someone he had met on a night out recently and he had read it by the morning light before he'd crept away. Oh, a night out, was it good? 1 asked, and he said, Yeah, it always is. You got lucky, 1 said, and he said, 1 always do. And he laughed. It always took me a second to remember that Will had other friends, or rather that he had a normal life full of normal things, and that it was 1 who was one of his other friends.

It had also rained hard on the day that we were arrested. That dawn. Sitting on the floor in front of the insurance company's office building with spray paint on our hands, cuffed to the suitcase we'd filled with cement, waiting to be arrested. Almost nobody on the street, but those that saw us gawked, took photos, heckled. 1 was wearing a surgical mask. Will wasn't. We'd got to recognise each other at actions and meetings and vigils but I only found out his name after we signed up to work together. Glass windows washed in paint, dripping into the gutters. In the dead hours, we talked in low tones about our child-hoods, our ideologies, the things we hoped would come to pass once the revolution came. Will said revolution without a single note of irony. He was the most nineteen-year-old person I'd ever met. He was reading Fanon. He was watching that new *Star Wars* show. His lecturers, he said, were ignorant. He was maybe going to drop out. I asked him what he would do instead, he shrugged. He was funny, he made me laugh as we got soaked beneath the awning of the building's entryway, as my teeth started to chatter. He said he spent every summer in Germany with his mum's family, he said Germany was so fucked. I said yeah, the art world was striking Germany, he said that was cool, it was good they were doing that. Then the cops came, and we were being filmed again, we started chanting. It was hard with just the two of us. Our voices kept going in and out of sync. *Intifada, revolution.* Our voices got hoarser. *Elbit kills kids.* We laid down on the wet asphalt, rainwater pouring into our noses and mouths. Cops grabbed our shoulders and pulled. At the station, we were searched, given baggy grey sweats to change into. Our paint-drenched jumpsuits and underlayers in different shades of black were sealed into plastic bags to stew all night, and by the time we got out they smelled so rotten that I would end up just throwing mine out. But at least we were warm in our cells and we even got given canvas slippers to wear to the interrogation rooms and back, which we'd take off and line up neatly just outside the doors of our cages, neighbours saying absent hellos.

My friend L. hadn't got that treatment when their encampment was swept early one morning by campus police. Every few weeks I sent L. a message on Signal that disappeared after an hour and that read, as casually as I could make it, *Checking in, are you ok?* and they would usually not reply. A few days after my dinner with Will I was scrolling my timeline and saw a four-second clip from a campus protest in America. On a paved path across a manicured lawn, in the soft sunshine, a swarm of cops milled about, helmets on their heads, guns in their holsters, batons strapped to their legs, one cop wearing this enormous shell-like backpack whose contents I couldn't begin to guess. The officers' bodies were bent low like they were looking for something that had fallen out of someone's pocket, a coin maybe. Only when the video looped back did I realise that they were making arrests. Students were lying face-down on their stomachs with their hands tied behind their backs, one of them prostrate, arms at an angle, wrists already swelling, I could tell from how red they looked. I hadn't noticed them at first. The one in the left side of the frame at the start of the shot, red and white keffiyeh over their face, lay so absolutely still that they looked dead. As the video played again, I watched their stiff and skinny body, unmoving, even as a cop, walking by, inadvertently kicked their baseball cap off their head and onto the ground. Their face pressed into the ground.

Already they were being made to disappear. I hadn't noticed them at first. The cops worked slowly. There were so many officers, four of them for each teenage faggot, full riot gear against woven cotton scarves. How many people had died begging for their lives just like this? Will had tried to kick one of the cops arresting us, the cop had only rolled his eyes. What had happened to Will and me had been mild compared to this. What was happening to these students was mild compared to what happened every minute of the day in Palestine, at checkpoints, on city streets, inside family homes. Why was I feeling this pang for the little gay-looking protester in the video who was so afraid that they couldn't even bring their body to tremble but who held a passport issued by the United States of America and who, tomorrow at the very latest, would find themself back in their bed with their bruises already fading?

Waiting to be arrested was the most difficult kind of wait, recounts the narrator of Rafeedie's *The Trinity of Fundamentals* as he hides behind a closet and listens to the Israeli occupation army beat down the doors of his safe house. After his nine long years in hiding, it takes them almost an hour to get to him, enough time for him to burn his papers and smoke one last cigarette. *They laid him face down on the ground after blindfolding him and tying his feet together with a zip tie similar to the one they had used to bind his hands.* At the monthly reading group I had read that part aloud and commented, But being caught is only the beginning of how it feels to be arrested. Nods on the Zoom call. It just wasn't the same.

After throwing up in the toilet bowl I messaged L.: *Checking in, just saw the walkout news, are you ok?* The video had only been posted two hours ago. I opened my laptop and went to the right-hand side of my Spotify page where I could see what songs all my friends had been listening to and when exactly. L.'s profile picture was their silhouette against a sunset in some mountain range. Eighteen hours ago they had been listening to Tracy Chapman. Evening in California, had they been on a run, at home with friends, studying in the library? What were they listening to now? There was only one tick on my message, meaning their phone was dead or turned off. *I love you*, I told L., followed by a million red heart emojis, *please let me know xxxxxxxxxxxxx*. L. would probably not reply, but the messages still had to be sent.

On the homepage of my Signal app, there were groups that I'd muted and my chat with Will, who had changed his username from Kindling to just the fire emoji. A coincidence: he was typing. He asked me if I was free to run reconnaissance on a building with him. It was a small museum that would soon be hosting a Christmas party for the employees of the company that leased office space to a UK contractor who made components for fighter jets. 29 October 2024: *UK's Lammy Defends 'Carve Out' Allowing F-35 Exports to Israel.* I said sure even though I thought it wasn't really that wise for the two of us, who had already been arrested together before, to be seen on the venue's CCTV only a few days before the event. Actually I thought it was stupid. But I said sure, I said I had the day off on Monday. Will said OK.

I ran into C. at the weekly vigil. She was bundled in a big winter coat, and after she finished handing out fake electric candles she wrapped an arm around me and gave me a side hug. I leaned against her. Someone started reading obituaries and she immediately began to cry loudly, heaving hiccups. People started glancing over at us. I rubbed my hand between her shoulder blades in circular motions and said, Shh, shh, but really I found myself repulsed by how public her grief was and how implicated I was in this performance, standing at her side, giving her my comfort, when neither she nor I had to worry about hearing the name of a family member dug out of the rubble in Gaza or attacked by settlers in the

West Bank. It was unfair to feel that way about C., I knew, but nothing about what was happening was fair.

Behind us in the busy thoroughfare a delivery rider zoomed past us on a motorcycle, Bluetooth speaker dangling from their backpack and blaring the chorus of a pop song. A siren somewhere a few streets over, long ululations floating into the distance. June Jordan: *I SAID I LOVED YOU AND I WANTED MUSIC OUT THE WINDOWS.*

Will came. Relief in my chest at the sight of him, his raised eyebrows by way of greeting, the rackety click-click-click of his freehub as he stopped pedalling, wove an arc around our group, and came to a slow stop behind C. and me. He gave C. a squeeze. She was shuddering, but she let Will loop his arm into hers. He bent to whisper something in her ear that seemed to help. I never knew what I was supposed to say when people were upset, I always fidgeted and wondered how I came across to others. I didn't know how Will could be so good at it when he was so young and naïve. Maybe because he cared so truly and deeply that it just came out of his body in exactly the right way. I didn't know where he got it from, the heart.

When I was let out of jail Will had already been released. I was told to leave via the back door at the end of a long linoleum corridor, and as soon as I stepped into the night he came running toward me and lifted me into the air. Did you also—? Did they ask you if—? He didn't answer, it wasn't safe to talk so close to the cop shop anyway. He jumped up and down and held me with such giddiness, as if I'd come back from the dead, as if my release were some unfathomable miracle, that I finally cried for the first time since it had all begun. After Will came my mother, who was furious, she had been raging hysterical all day. I hadn't told her beforehand. I was glad I'd been unreachable during the worst parts of her crisis. Will and I took a picture holding the red, white, green and black flag of Palestine—*Actionists released after...*—and said hi to the comrades who'd volunteered for police station support, who'd brought thermoses and camping chairs and the phones we'd stashed with them before the action. Will got along with my mother, had helped calm her down before I came out. He didn't complain.

We ended up staying in a Holiday Inn nearby that my mother had booked, me and her on the big bed and Will on the floor, and the next morning as we were checking out she started begging me to come home with her, just for a while, just until I felt better. I was mortified. Rafeedie's mother had said to him, *Go, my son, may God be pleased with you.* It was what had kept him alive. I pried her off my forearm, finger by finger. Later, when Will and I were on the train and my mother was supposed to be at work, she called me on the phone crying again, saying last night Will had told her that I was a lesbian, was that true? Tell me where I went wrong, she wailed, tell me how I failed as a parent. I didn't say anything back. The phone was pressed to my ear but everyone in the quiet carriage could hear. Will pretended not to, instead handing me a part of the tangerine he'd been peeling, and I felt that nobody in my life had ever been so kind to me. Fragments of landscape sped away from us behind windowpanes streaked with the dried outlines of another day's rain. June Jordan: *the blossoming flamingos of my wild mimosa trees.* After the long silence listening to my mother's weeping I hung up and Will extended his palm to me. I put my phone in his hand, he put my phone in his pocket, and I had the last of the tangerine.

When the vigil ended, Will whispered to me. I'd lost feeling in the tips of my fingers, I was so cold. Do you want to get a drink after this? he said. C. had stopped crying but her nose was red and her lips were chapped. She looked ugly, she was an ugly crier. The way her lips curdled pulled at her nose and flattened the whole of her face into a cowpat. C. wiped her nose with her coat sleeve and unfolded her tote bag. My stomach heavy with dread. She was about to go collect all the candles again and everyone would see on her face how upset she was. People we'd never met. They'd comfort her and feel bad for her, for C. I didn't know the right way to tell her that she needed to stop making everything about herself. It would only make me the bad guy. I said to Will, No, I'm good.

More attendance than usual this week and now they were getting ready to go back to their lives, their limbs stirring again, murmurs of conversation. C. thanked each of them for their solidarity. Someone had brought their dog, a small black thing with ears jutting up and a padded winter vest, and I thought of Mohammad Bhar, the young man with Down syndrome who said, Khalas, ya habibi, khalas, as he reached out to pet the beast that was killing him. The love in his heart.

The museum was made out of a townhouse that had once been home to a rich merchant in the eighteenth century. He had accumulated a tasteful art collection and personal library, with books and paintings and prints lining every wall, even busts in alcoves along the staircases, a drawing room with armchairs that said *Please do not sit*. When I arrived, Will was holding a pair of tickets to the guided group tour. He said it was only £5 for students, and he

24

said it was a good thing I was late because they'd tried to ask to see my student ID too but didn't because of the rush. I was miffed. I wasn't that late. It was only 11:03.

The tour's started already, Will said, come on.

He bundled me inside and kept chattering as he loped after me, hands shoved deep into his pockets. I held my breath walking past the security guard, but he didn't stop to check my bag. I was relieved even though there wasn't anything bad inside it. I thought maybe he could tell I was jittery. I looked for cameras without craning my neck so much I'd be obvious. The house was narrow, cramped, and the tour group took up all the space, pushing against the other guests, intruding upon their quiet. At least two cameras and a docent per room, no service entrances—it had to be a nightmare to clean. The guide took us up the winding staircases and showed us sliding panels specially constructed for the room of Venetian canalscapes, here was a bustling summer afternoon, here was golden hour on St Mark's Square, see the light streaming through the translucency of the watercolour. Will made a whole show of stroking his chin as he listened to the guide, brows furrowed and nodding. Once upon a time I cared about this shit. Part of me still did. I read the signs out of habit and tried to imagine what it would be like to stand here one evening with a flute of prosecco in one hand and the other picking canapés from trays. I wanted to scream.

We went down all the stairs again and the guide took us into the courtyard where the sky was grey and low. The café was open. Outdoor tables and chairs. The group started to disperse, some of them lining up to ask questions of the guide, others to revisit the rooms, and the rest just standing there, checking their phones, waiting for someone to tell them what to do. A gust of wind sent my hair flying into my face, strands sticking to the chapstick on my lips.

Will paced around suspiciously, back and forth, back and forth. Then, giving me a certain kind of look, he said, I need to pee, don't you?

There was so much pent-up energy inside me, enough to climb onto a roof, tackle a security guard to the ground, swing a sledgehammer. I nodded.

I went with him to the toilets, through the hall and down the stairs, a converted pantry with two stalls. He ducked into the left and I went into the right. Instead of peeing I put the toilet lid down and climbed on top of it, teetering, never not anxious that I was going to break something. The tank was fixed high up on the wall. I had stickers in my pocket, black and red with the words *Palestine will never die.* I peeled one off and was reaching up to post it on the toilet tank when there was a loud blaring behind me. I almost slipped and fell, my hand shot out to the grimy wall. The fire alarm. For a delirious second I thought maybe it was me that had set it off somehow. It kept going as I paused to catch my breath. Will, I whispered or hissed, Will, Will, but there was no response. I hadn't heard the door open or shut or anything. But when I emerged into the hand-washing area there was nobody there, and the cubicle was empty. He was gone.

All the visitors pouring out of the museum and onto the street. A staff member in a neon marshal jacket saying it was all going to be okay, to please keep calm. I couldn't see Will, he would be head and shoulders over everyone else if he were still in the crowd. I wondered if he had pulled the alarm but I couldn't think of a single reason why. My head swivelling. The street now full and passers-by staring at us, sounds of the city suddenly too much to bear, the train track on the overpass nearby rattling and rumbling. If you're looking for your friend, said someone who'd been on the tour with us, I think he's just left.

What? I said. I must have looked annoyed because the person's expression changed and they shrugged and walked off. All the visitors were streaming off now, they couldn't be bothered to wait for the situation to be fixed, it was just the staff members left, huddled together, and some people looking at Google Maps. None of them wanted to help me.

I felt in my tote bag for my phone, it was slippery with the sweat of my palms. Signal—notifications clogged my homepage and I couldn't find Will's account anywhere. I thought maybe he had blocked me until I saw him in a list of group chat members and he'd changed his username again. Now it was '(A)', the little fucker. Fingers shaking, I typed *??????????* and *where are you?!?!*

His reply came instantly: *ahh something came up.* I asked him what the whole toilet thing was about, surely it had been code for something, he'd been asking me for something, I wanted to know why he had looped me in just to ditch me, I was baffled, why would he do that? *I'm going off grid for a bit*, he said, and I could feel them, my thoughts slipping around in my mind like soup in a takeout container, lapping against the sides of my skull. I could feel myself going crazy.

I tried calling him but he rejected it—
I'm on a train
I couldn't understand.
Are we still doing the action here ?!
I think I can't anymore this time but you totally should if you want / ill be gone for a while / but ill see you when im back / will tell you about it then
    what???

27

Standing there on the pavement, blocking the way, with my phone gripped in both hands, I felt as though my soul were leaving my body. My arms and legs felt thick and heavy but the inside of me was peeling itself away and floating upwards into the sky. I didn't know what to do. I felt hysterical, I was devastated, I almost wanted to call the police, ring someone, anyone, and say... what? There's been a—I, I lost—ah, a friend of mine left without saying goodbye. I didn't know why I was so upset. He said he would be coming back. Why was my heart breaking, seizing in my chest? Tears spilling out of my eyes, snot in my throat, great big snorts as I gasped for breath. Then it hit me all at once. I was behaving like my mother. *After what your father did, this is how you punish me.* I froze. Bending over, I tried to make myself stop crying. People passing by looked for my face before moving on. I couldn't make words, I wanted to tell them I was fine, it was fine.

But that jolt, the disgust of recognition, I didn't know what to do with it. Sometimes I felt that way, like I was slobbering. Like I was a dog locked in a cage in a big empty house, unable to understand, barking and barking until my master came home.

Will was on a train somewhere, switching between tabs on his phone, hoodie up, leaning back into the plastic seat, legs splayed open and taking up all the space around him, and thinking hard, as always. Wherever it was he was going, some part of him had to be excited, it was urgent, it was daring, it was bigger than himself. He was such a guy. It was such a white guy thing to do. He didn't have to answer to anyone. He didn't care about school. He didn't care about himself. Was he supposed to care what I thought.

I thought about throwing my phone into traffic, smashing it against the brick wall until its shards made my fingers bleed. I thought about quitting everything. I thought about killing myself. Then he'd see. But I didn't. I said to Will, *this really fucking sucks*, and I walked to the bus stop and waited eight minutes for the next bus to come, and out of habit took a sticker out of my pocket and tacked it on the pole where the timetable was posted. I didn't care who saw me. They could try to tell me off for putting up a single sticker with a message that reminded them of how complacent they all, we all were. What were they gonna do.

L. finally replied, their messages coming to me in the middle of the night.
   i'm fine
   beat up by cops and held in a cell overnight lol
   Then, three minutes after that:
   how r u?
   ily2

After a few weeks passed, it occurred to me to try and track down where Will lived, but his housemates didn't know where he'd gone either. There was a subletter in his room and they'd put most of his stuff in the closet, I was welcome to root through it if I wanted, but I thought it best not to. I tried to imagine him living in that rank student flat with these other first-years. It wasn't exactly hard to. The housemates were being standoffish and shy, I wondered if they thought I was a cop, if I looked like I could be a cop. Back home, scrolling Instagram, Twitter and Telegram, I looked for him in every picture of every protest, was that his gangly body folded up into itself at this die-in, was that his voice in the chant of the crowd? Or maybe it was that I had done something wrong, that I'd been too much, he'd felt suffocated. If so, god, I was sorry. I kept opening our history on Signal and typing out messages to him and deleting them, resentful. The conversations from before were long gone. One-hour timer. Opsec. And in the meantime, more bombs, more rubble, more deaths, more crowdfunders, more begging for money and attention and a fraction of fucking empathy, real things to grieve. I made myself move on, dragged my exhausted body to work and to actions and meetings and refrained from asking about him. If he had something to say, he would say it.

Then came the bombing attempt in Germany. It had gone off in front of the embassy but it hadn't done much damage. The authorities were offering rewards for information leading to arrest. Politicians issued emotional statements even though nobody had died. On social media, people with watermelon emojis in their display names were saying that things had gone too far, or things were being set back, or, or, or. I had to delete all the apps from my phone. I was numb, like I wasn't even part of the world, like my skin wasn't in contact with the air around it, like everything was muffled, the soundwaves, the quality of the light. In my bedroom with the curtains drawn I lay on my back with my hands clasped against my stomach and turned the news over and over in my head, getting angrier as I did. Who cared what these people thought, on the internet, where they could say what they wanted. They didn't know, they had nothing to do with it. I did. I knew. Will—it had to have been. He was so fucking stupid. I couldn't know what he had been thinking. Well, actually, I could and I did. All the time.

C. came over after my shift ended. She told me that he was going to be okay, as if she knew something I didn't. I said he's just a fucking kid. I thought about what I would buy him if he ended up in prison. What I'd be allowed to send. Where they'd even put him. I wished C. would give me my book back. Again I told C. the story about the train. C. said, He can be a real asshole. I said, One time we went wheatpasting in the middle of the night and thought we saw a cop car cruising by so we legged it and he was still holding the Tupperware box of paste and ended up with it all over the front of his jacket that he never was able to wash out.

Even though we were laughing together and I was pouring her tea and we were listening to Tracy Chapman, something had changed after that vigil. I didn't like to see C. happy, I didn't like to see her sad, I realised that I just didn't like her anymore. The false innocence of her face, the way it had bloomed red splotches when she'd cried, like some pungent flower beckoning the bees to come. Actually I despised her. I never wanted to see her again. But I knew I wasn't supposed to feel that way. I couldn't tell anyone. Not even Will. Or I would, if somehow that was the thing that would bring him back. But anyway who cared, who cared where Will had gone? Things like this happened every day. Were happening now. Will wasn't special. None of us were. C. and I were planning something new, not arrestable, not for now. Maybe one day years down the line we'd meet again, Will and me, in a better kind of world, as better kinds of people. Or maybe not.

❦

Before Will left, I had a dream about him. My friends and I were in the top floor of a building that we had occupied, looking out of the windows with our hands obscuring the bottom half of our faces. In case of cameras. I spotted Will downstairs, saw him walk across the courtyard towards us. It was what he was wearing. Starched white shirt, tailored black jacket, the trousers with the crease ironed down the middle of each leg. Shoes shined. He shouted at us and ordered us to leave the building. The group that was with him, dressed the same, they hooted and hollered, broke into jeering chants. We ceded the building to him, creeping out the back door. When I woke up from that dream I felt devastated—not because he had hurt me but because I had seen him wearing a suit. Will, a friend of mine. He would be so embarrassed. It was worse than seeing him naked. It was worse than seeing him dead.

—*October–November 2024*

This story is a work of fiction. Any resemblance to real events, organisations or people is coincidental and unintentional.

I am indebted to: SW (!), EY, AT, LS, RW, VD, EC, MW, AD, AC, HW, LM, CY, EK, HYZ, Mohammed El-Kurd, Wisam Rafeedie (and Dr Muhammad Tutunji and Palestinian Youth Movement), June Jordan, and everyone who has taken direct action in solidarity with Palestine.

Glory and eternity to the martyrs.

A version of this story was originally self-published in November 2024 in a limited-edition hand-bound risograph pamphlet.

All proceeds from this story are split evenly between the following two families in Gaza:

Mahmoud Nasser, twenty-four, from Beit Hanoun, northern Gaza, is the sole breadwinner for twenty family members. In 2023, the IOF destroyed Mahmoud's home, and their family has been displaced at least five times. Donate to Mahmoud's family's daily survival needs at **bit.ly/4be5H5i**.

Hossam, fifteen, urgently needs open heart surgery, for which he is trying to get special permission to leave Gaza. His family also needs funds for their daily survival needs. Donate to Hossam and his family at **tinyurl.com/hossamchuffed**.

Please also visit **gazafunds.com** for more Gaza fundraisers in need.

AMERICAN SONNET, AFTER TERRENCE HAYES

Malika McKenney

Song: Mitski – 'Buffalo Replaced'

Look at me, trying to write you an American sonnet,
part wild red buffalo, part vanishing white lie,
where I restrain the beast, then try my hardest to hold it,
look into its darkening darting wet eyes,
reach down past sick gums to a hell-burning throat,
feel it pulling my hand and my hair and my heart,
and while trapped there between dulling teeth and the world,
ask it once, twice, three times about faith, about God,
about fighting and falling, about fields, about floods,
about freedom mixed up with dark animal cud,
about dreaming—you've seen it, buried deep in its gut—
but my fist comes up empty, holding nothing but blood.

So I get out my gun of American steel,
shoot it once, twice, three times, let it see how it feels.

DISS TRACK SONNET

Christian Yeo Xuan

Song: Saint Levant feat. MC Abdul – 'Deira'

lord, let the blues poison my body or let me inherit
my mother's generous eyes. the oeuvre of personable
people is made up of toes. softness lies between them
the toes. i've always known there was something rabid
about me, her calculation and his rage live inside me like
a blowtorch. who said the sonnet is a good form for a
psycho. who said you can't wreak that much damage in
fourteen lines. fuck, what have i done. fourteen lines all
it takes, keeps taking. implicate the self. am afraid. am
honest. okay. i'll add the 'i'. *i* keep taking. *i* blowtorch.
i shit the blues. yeah last year i sat in a lecture, your face
printing my pocket. lecture said, get in there and change
your mind. i couldn't even change my spit. now we're here
at last. no volta, no curtain, animal. *god, sonnet, save me, i*

IN THE ABSENCE, FIRE

Malak Hijazi

Song: Julia Boutros – 'Thoouar Al Ardh – ثوّار الأرض'

I was born in a refugee camp, where houses were packed together like sardine cans, each holding not only bodies but the stories of entire villages and cities, compressed into concrete. These houses—once tents—were meant to be temporary, but over time, the camp became permanent.

From my window, I could see into the lives of my neighbours. My friend across the alley would be waking up, her mother's voice echoing through the walls. I'd smirk and say sarcastically, 'The princess just woke up.' Our lives touched without our trying. The walls were too thin to hold back voices, and sometimes I could hear arguments, laughter and the clinking of teacups. Privacy was a myth, but so was loneliness. We were part of each other's days.

I thought the world must have been like mine—the zebra-printed uniforms, the forty-five students in each classroom, the canteen selling sugar-water labelled as juice. I never brought food from home—it was embarrassing, even though we were all refugees, all poor. At the time, I didn't understand we were marked under a category. I thought of myself as ordinary, even boring.

The word 'refugee' was written on the walls of my school, but I didn't know its weight. One day, a teacher asked about my family's original hometown, and I went home to ask my mother. She gave me a name that sounded like a secret—half-story, half-spell. I couldn't

39

picture it. It didn't live in my memory, nor fully in hers, or even in her mother's. My grandmother was still in her mother's womb during the Nakba, carried in the body of a woman who had no time to say goodbye to the land she fled. She didn't realise it was a final departure. Not even in her darkest thoughts did she imagine the almond tree she had planted would one day be harvested by someone from Poland, Russia or Morocco.

But the wound remained. The feeling of being less—because we had no home—hung in the air. The weight of loss settled into our lives like dust in the corners of our fragile houses. We were a word written before we were born—refugee—an identity imposed, printed on the UNRWA ration card, carried like a birthmark.

I grew up just 12 kilometres away from that village, but reaching the moon felt more possible. I was a fallaha, a villager, but I didn't know what that meant until a girl from Jaffa told me she was from a 'real city'.

'You're just from a village,' she said, 'working in the fields.'

It was funny because we didn't even have a garden, and my father didn't know how to plant a seed.

So I looked for myself in schoolbooks and scraps of old Palestinian poems. I pieced together my identity from other people's metaphors. I learned the names of places we no longer saw, and people we no longer met. I clung to phrases like 'tying the train with ropes' as if I had lived them myself.

The news lingered like background noise. My father always had it on. I heard the word 'occupation' before I could spell it. I knew what a refugee camp was before I could name mine. I learned the difference between a refugee and a 'Gazan original', between an airstrike and a detonation. I understood that there were people who wanted Gaza burned off the map. But back then, it just felt like the way the world worked.

Rage didn't come from missiles or the daily news of killings. Not at first. It came quietly, slowly—when I began to understand the world's order. I started noticing the lives depicted on screens and in illustrated stories: films where kids ran through autumn leaves, where school buses were yellow and wide, and every child had a house with a garden to return to. I wondered how they never had to shout over airstrikes or count bullet holes in the walls. Our world was different—one where we joked about Israeli drones watching our dances, our tongues stuck out in defiance.

Even bedtime stories betrayed me. My sister read me tales of girls visiting grandmothers in the countryside, where rivers ran clear, where wolves in red cloaks were the greatest danger. No one fled a village, no one lost a home. There were no words for tank treads, checkpoints, blood or bullets. I remember staring at the illustrations—hills, forests, wide skies—and wondering, is this how paradise looks?

That realisation deepened when I heard adults say the very things killing us were made in the U.S. They lived untouched, indifferent to the life we clung to. In 2009, I was ten. I watched Condoleezza Rice keep her hand down—choosing not to stop the war on Gaza. Her silence was louder than any vote. The tiny life I clung to—hiding under the bed, in the cupboard, fearing a bomb—was too much for the world to spare. That's when it began.

I understood then that our survival is treated as disposable. We're not meant to exist in their world, but we are here. Still here. Still holding on to what they couldn't take, still telling stories in a world that refuses to listen.

When I write about how our story began with exile, Western audiences are often astonished. As if history doesn't exist until it's spoon-fed to them. I remember speaking to an American editor who exclaimed, 'OMG, that's a story!' I had always known my life had narrative value, but she needed to be astonished. It wasn't her astonishment that compelled me to write. It was the agony of not having the ordinary. The birthmark inherited from my ancestors, the thoughts lodged in my throat since birth.

Lately, I'm tired. Tired of how every event in our lives must be made exotic. Tired of serving up grief in prose. I envy those whose names are never in the news. I seek the ease of being unnoticed. I dream of the ordinary. But history won't let me have it.

I remember the first time I googled the name of our village. I expected paradise—the kind my grandparents described in their stories. But all I found were faded images: deserted houses and yellowing fields. Why did I expect more? Because the stories were always about people—their laughter, their arguments, their everyday lives. Not ruins. The stories had created something real in my mind—a living, breathing place. They planted a dream of an alternative future, one where the past wasn't lost, where the people remained.

And in that dream, I dared to ask: What if?

It was then that I realised what makes a space truly a place is not the land or the buildings, but the people—the heart within it. The photographs felt alien, for they were empty of those I had imagined. Stripped of living memory, the village was no longer mine. Without us, it had lost its essence, becoming nothing but a shadow of what it could have been. That's why it pains me so deeply when people are killed in this ongoing genocide. What is home without its people?

In Gaza, everything bears witness to this truth. Even the stones we walk on carry our pain. Our loss is embedded in the concrete beneath our feet, the names of martyrs written in blood and memory. These names cannot be erased. They haunt the walls, the streets, the corners of our minds. Every name is a fire, every memory is resistance.

Golda Meir once said, 'The old will die, and the young will forget.' They bet on our silence. But the old have passed, and the young have not forgotten. We've etched memory into the very walls, into our names, into the rhythm of our feet as we walk streets we've never seen. They fear our memory, because they know they cannot extinguish it.

I know it's become cliché to say we resist through story-telling. But I write not for relief, but because this is what they didn't expect: that we would keep telling it. That we would keep remembering. That we would resist the urge to make our rage poetic—and instead, let it smoulder. Let it burn through the absence. Let it create space where the world tried to erase us.

I will never romanticise it. Blood is red, and that's not poetic. Fire melts human flesh, and there's nothing inspiring about it. The reality is wild and bleak. There's no art in screams, no metaphor in the silence of graves.

The world may try to dress it up—make it distant, digestible—but the truth is bare, brutal and close. The stories they want—those that sell—aren't the ones we live. Our truth isn't for comfort or applause. It wasn't written for film festivals or publishing houses. If anything must wake you, let it not be sympathy. Let it not be pity.

Let it be rage. Rage that unsettles. Rage that refuses silence. Rage that tears through the lies and forces you to see us—not as metaphors, not as shadows, not as a lesson in someone else's curriculum, but as people the world is actively trying to erase.

And if you think you can build distance, craft an architecture to shield your eyes from the wreckage, convince yourself the violence is far away—then believe this: the same system will one day reach you. What devours us now will hunger for you later—if not in blood, then in silence, numbness, or the slow decay of all that makes you human.

You are not safe in your forgetting.

And we are not gone.

THINKING ABOUT RAPE IN THE COURTYARD OF A COFFEESHOP

Bidhya Limbu

Song: Gil Scott-Heron – 'The Revolution Will Not Be Televised'

There is not escape as much as there is sitting in open sunlight reliving everything. No new body, no new life. There aren't even new stories, just the same archive in perfectly inconsiderate containers. There is only watching something resembling an egg hurtling off a balcony at full speed. When I was thirteen, I sprained my ankle on a concrete court for the first time. I was out of the game for weeks, but not a day longer than necessary. You would not have met a teenager more dedicated to recovery. I would not have let a wounded leg steal time. Still, last week, my ankle gave way while I was walking on solid ground. I understand. The only guarantee is the small shell of tragedy that lies medium dead in my body at all times. The threat of wheels hitting tarmac and the plane bursting into flames, even after cruising through all that sky. If I am afraid of dying it is only because of what it will do to Christian or Laetitia. Impossibly, there are still bodies I have to tend to. In this way, I am not a poet of desecration, or betrayal, or even orphanage. I am a poet the way a survivor is not a near miss, the way tossing a body off a cliff is not a through-road. I am even a poet the way a song is not a songbird. The possibility of softness insists on itself. That is why I am still here. Yield as revolt to the good evil you feel you deserve. Trust what gathers around a table. Poetry feels like I am seven and by the beach with my older brother again. We overturn rock after smoothened rock, waiting for a crab to scuttle free. One more critter of memory. Another crustacean bearing the blueprint of our family home. Reclamation is carolling my younger selves into a car and taking them to homes of devotion rather than safety. Granting my brother an unsullied future. Kernelling my abuser's teeth. Attrition and uncertainty, until my mother calls my name from the other room—when I enter, she is sitting across my long-distance lover, asking me what the word for *yungngese* is in English. *Stay*, I say. The word is, *stay*.

Anthony keep loving & raging MB

APPLICATION FOR SOCIAL HOUSING IN TOWER HAMLETS

Mymona Bibi

Song: Pan Sonic – 'Urania'

Please fill in BLOCK CAPITALS

First name: Surname:

Other names: Date of birth:

Address: Postcode:

Are you
– subject to immigration control?
– under 18?
– not living in the borough?
– not in housing need?
– guilty?
– receiving an income of more than £90,000 per annum?
– a homeowner?

Please circle the appropriate answer.

Does the ceiling you're under ever leak and cave when your eyes are closed?

Yes   No   Not sure   My eyes are always open.

47

How many rooms do you need to store all your nightmares?

I   2   3   4   Other

Have you or any members of your household slept through the night in this house? (not including the voices)

Yes   No   Not sure   My eyes are always open.

Where are your children? And where have they been whilst you've been filling out this form?

> They are everywhere spilling from bed to toilet to street, their screams are almost as loud as the letterbox clicking shut behind the neatly folded bills. Will this envelope be big enough to seal me and them and all this noise until the cladding is removed?

BROKEN PARROT: WARRIOR TONGUE

Simran Kaur Johal

Song: Sampha – 'Blood On Me'

KID IN A CANDY STORE

I'm just a kid in a candy store, lost and looking for something I can't find. It's an aching feeling that makes me want to cry. I wish I knew what it was. I want to ask the sales assistant for the shelf, the aisle, the store. But I'm just a kid in a candy store, lost and looking for something I can't find.

I'm small looking for big things: why do I want to own it all? My mum likes to remind me, I won't have anywhere to put everything, but somehow I'd like to know I could shove it away, instead of all that empty space under my bed—better than the monsters.

I'm just a kid in a candy store, and I grew up. But I never lost the desperate tantrum. It lives on, mean and hungry in my sneering lip. Never got what I wanted. Never knew what I wanted. Just knew that I wanted. Now I feel unwanted. This makes me all shades of stupid—I can't tell if the lighter or darker fits me better. Does this kind of thing go with a scarf and my curly hair? Does it match the frenzy of being twenty? I don't need to worry about which way to go, I just need to go.

But for some reason I can't move my feet. For some reason I'm stood still and the whole world is moving around me. I'm seeing everything on the spinning atlas, and I can't take any of it in, without it feeling like I'm a looter. The stars? I want to steal them to have a sparkle in these brown eyes. The people walking past red buses and zebra crossings? I want to put them in a poster, hang them on my wall. What a loser. Desire-filled; empty-headed. Cold in a sauna, laying on the ground while I'm falling through the sky.

MEANING DISEASE

'Wake up,' my dad tells me. And I turn to look at him, spoon of cereal crackling in my mouth, hair dishevelled and pyjamas still on. *What the hell does he mean?* Maybe he's onto something. In what ways am I not awake? Let me think. No point. So I tell my dad with all of my wakefulness, 'My eyes are open.'

He laughs at me, patting my head, 'It has to mean something to be awake. Opening your eyes? You think that's all it takes?' *Why yes, I do.* I don't understand him. Damn. Maybe he's on something, not onto something. So I close my eyes, really tight. Then I open them again. 'Yeah, I'm pretty sure,' I tell him. Probably some kind of old age disease, this meaning thing. But I think I'm getting a tickle in my throat.

EDINBURGH ‹ — › LONDON

April. Edinburgh. II AM. There's me walking through it. I wonder if it matters that I'm here—and where does all that mattering go? In its medieval buildings, its pissed-on walls, the people in Princes Street Gardens? Nah. I don't think so. Then again, if that building, that wall, those people, that park can matter to me, maybe I stand a chance while I'm waiting at the crossing. Did anyone look at me and notice? That I'm a just a kid in a candy store, lost and looking for something I can't find.

April. Edinburgh. 7 PM. Coughed my way around the city, kept on taking trains at Waverley just to learn my own name. Wondered about how my face looks to the people on the platform, in the window of a carriage pulling away. Is she funny? Is she sad? Is she dreaming? Is she fighting? I hope she's a funny fighter. Tongue out, eyes crossed. That's the real ticket. Into where? I'm not sure—when it matters, I'll let you know. And I hope no one saw just how taken I was with my own reflection, smiling at the faded image of me instead of those houses and hills. I forgot the world when I stood before it. I'm just a kid in a candy store, lost and looking for something I can't find, and sometimes I wonder if that thing might be me. But that's not quite right.

June. London. 5 PM. I'm on the train home and every time this thought occurs, *why does this feel like the beginning of a film?* Then I think about how there's no plot, and I see why films like to cut and fade to black—that's what's happening here. All these small moments might mean something, these instances might finally be what I've been looking for. So I hang on to these things: me walking with a suitcase and three bags dangling off my shoulders, me drinking coffee by a window with a good view. *You don't know how good things are about to get.*

Bag snaps off my shoulders, view gets ruined by a face that I know. *Fin. Fade to black. Roll the credits. There's only one name. No one remembers it.* I'm told I should pay attention to the signs regardless, notice the moments when life is on my side. Religiously, I make eleven elevens. Nothing happens. These angel numbers, I should just be grateful—is that how it is?

August. London. 8 PM. The sound of the rain in my already soaked brain. Takes nothing to make a puddle in this place. Words are over and on my head—like flies on a lion's face. In Metropolis Desert, I am prowling through the busyness of a city where nothing is actually happening. Summer is gone and my eyes were barely open. I'm always exhausted, still lost and looking for something I just can't find. I need a summer for the summer.

September. Edinburgh. 10 AM. It's uneven but here I am. I am here. As I walk through Nicolson Street on the way to my new flat, I read the graffiti on a wall lined with bins, *Where the lost things go, they grow.*

SPEAK-NOT-SO-EASY

Let me tell you about an anger I have. It's so serious that it can't be spoken.

Before reaching my new flat I am knocked into a million times by tourists, given dirty looks because the locals think I am a tourist too with these bags and my sunglasses sliding down my nose. Is a student still a tourist? *Maybe.* This wouldn't mean too much if it wasn't for the flashing image of me past shop windows, sweaty and brown in all of this white. I wish I weren't so paranoid all the time, that me walking to my new flat could just be part of the hustle and bustle. But why does that man's stare feel charged? Why is it that when I'm waiting at the bus stop, messy hair and badly buttoned shirt, that I feel like I'm an animal to them? I keep wiping sweat, wishing I could wipe myself off of myself while I'm at it. *Why do I do this?*

All day I wrack my brain for it. I try to write the prettiest lines with the longest words. But I can never say what I mean. I try and play this game at these points, where I can excuse myself. *Well, this isn't my language or country anyway, I only live in Empire Island, I'm not actually part of it.* Then again, I know more English than Punjabi, so what am I even talking about? And I'm here right now, I've always been here, so why can't I be part of it? *I'm a joke to where I'm from, colourful contradictions that they don't want to get to know. I'm a mime in the now where I am, drawing invisible boxes, and banging against thin air.* That's not it. I smack my lips and curse my tongue.

When I'm opening the door to my flat I immediately notice what's outside the window across the street. I don't take in any of the rooms, or check if anyone else has moved in. In the window of another person I'm seeing something that just can't be ignored. I drop my bags and forget that I need to pee, sticking my hands against the window to watch.

There is a parrot sitting in a brown cage. It's green like the colour of grass but its stomach is a burnt-orange sand from Mars. It has a big pink carnation in its beak, and at first I thought the Parrot and its blushing pink flower was a pretty picture. But she's making a face that's sort of horrifying. Her eyes are crossed and she is constantly darting them around; her tongue has fallen and flopped out of her mouth, wriggling from time to time, under and over the flower. I stay at the window for a while, just watching the strange Parrot. And I'm pretty sure she's watching me.

Let me tell you, this anger that I have, it's so serious that it's silly, so it's never spoken.

GIMMICK

Morning is a broken time of day, and I'm broken in it. Most of the time I'm fine, things are good, things are bad.

I can keep up with the pace, the ebb, the flow. But in the morning—I'm indescribable. Some days I wake up, I get that crushing feeling, and then I don't get up until 3 PM.

The only way I will get up is for the gimmick. I recently discovered that the more I try and look like them, the more I learn the art of blending in, the easier it is to sit in rooms with them, wait at stoplights next to them. It's just—I think I've gone too far with it. I'm enjoying it too much. Fashion was never such an interest until it was on me, until I started thinking *maybe I'm beautiful.*

Today, when I wake up my head feels like a fallen-down snow globe, and I'm convinced it's not worth it. What do I do in a day? Whom do I matter to in a day? But then I remember that wine-coloured dress I want to wear, and that butterfly clip I like to pin up in my curls. Now it's worth it. It's not like anyone will notice or stop to stare, but I will. I'll have something good to look at while I'm walking those long walks past shop windows, staring into the blank screen of my laptop.

I'm making my bed while yawning earth-shattering yawns in the cold morning, when I see something staring at me through my window. Beady eyes, silly smile— the Parrot. She traces my steps, imitating me along the window's ledge, like she wants to become me. *Pet parrots aren't allowed out of their cages like this, are they?* I shoo her away, wondering if I'm making her up. I think about this as I head to the bathroom, still groggy and fuzzy.

With the weight of the day already on me I press my hands into my eyes, and I'm so close to screaming. So close. *But no one will hear, and if they realise I made that sound, they'll move on.* I wash my face with some vigour now, trying to get rid of these thoughts. While I wet my hair to sort the curls out, my fingers get stuck in a tangle, and I'm so close. I'm so close to just ripping it all out. *It doesn't matter. It doesn't matter. Whatever I do to myself is a boomerang, it just comes back to me.* I shake my head with mousse running through it, hoping, just hoping these thoughts get shaken out too. The Parrot is still there imitating me, shaking her head like I am, as if she's got curly hair on that green head. She's making me laugh, cracking the sour mould on my morning face.

My window is open ever so slightly so I wonder if she'll imitate my voice too. I try a simple 'hello'. She doesn't imitate this though. Instead she screeches so loud I jump out of the skin I just moisturised and stuck down to myself. At this, I decide to properly shoo her away, my face lowered to hers, aiming to scare her. She doesn't flinch one bit; instead she gets even closer to the window and squawks. Funnily enough, I squawk back, finding something tempting about screeching noise. Is this violence or a strange kind of love? I can't tell.

Hooking my necklace in and rubbing perfume into my wrists, I feel slightly soothed. I like what I'm looking at. The way the dress fits around my waist, the way it complements the silver necklace, the way my hair is parted off to the side, with a small butterfly hair clip tucked behind my ear. For one minute I am happy. Because maybe dressed like this I'm allowed to be here. Maybe I can walk in life today like they do. I look at the Parrot and she stops imitating me, just stares at me with her tongue flopped out of her beak.

When I'm on my way to my first class of the day, I notice how I stand out. I overcorrected. It's a bit too much for the grey weather, especially that wine colour, and the purple butterfly in my hair. Travelling circus. Maybe it would be okay on someone else, but not on me—this parroting is reverb on me.

The next day, I'm in Lidl and immediately distracted by the bakery section. While I'm deciding on my sweet treat, I feel policed. I consider it being my own conscience at first. But I don't think my conscience is a white woman in a trench coat. And if it is, that's pretty fucked up. This white woman is looking at me with the most venomous stare, up and down while I'm reaching for a doughnut. I say 'excuse me' trying to get past her and she just stands there like a statue, glaring at me. *Damn.* 'There's more doughnuts,' I tell her, attempting to calm this aimless anger she has. Then, in the aisle with rice and canned goods, I see a girl I know from film society and decide to wave at her, but she's with her white friends, so she looks mortified at the sight of me. So, quickly, a supermarket becomes another place for me to keep my head down. Always interesting—the ones who collect you, then treat you like a one-night stand. There's a hierarchy here, carefully stacked and constantly wobbling, but a hierarchy nonetheless.

I'm about to pay when something happens. With my miscellaneous items I'm struggling along to the queues; I didn't get a basket because I honestly thought I only needed two things, but it piled up. And suddenly my boots give out, and I fall flat on my face. When I fall I bite my tongue, and I'm laying there with what feel like snapped ankles. Once you've fallen down, you'd think there's nothing left to lose, but it's the getting up that kills even more.

Nobody offers to help me up; they just stare like that white woman, statues, and I'm pretty sure a kid kicked me just now. An image is suddenly stuck in my mind: the Parrot. My eyes are printing those wings and that beak

56

out onto my pages—crossed eyes, limp tongue, pink carnation in her mouth. And then me—bitten tongue, snapped ankles, doughnut in my tilted Jenga-game jaw.

BITE OF A BUTTERFLY

I'm walking around at night, wondering what to do with myself in this dress I've got on. It feels like I need to be something, and not at any point in the future. Just right now. Right now I need to be something. I stop by the window of a car to look at myself, and there's a wickedness to me staring back at me, it's something I've been doing a lot lately. I just want to undress and check which parts are fuckable. Like lightning flashes I'm alive, appearing and then disappearing under my shirts and skirts.

This way that I look at myself, it will happen anywhere and all the time. I'll notice a smell like honey on my warmed skin out in a park where I'm reading. Then I'll put my fist against my cheek, pressing it hard, like a punch in slow motion while I think about being touched. I rub my eyes and leave my book hanging open on my thigh.

I'm the mess on my fifteen-year-old self's desk. Hubba Bubba packs left open, empty Victoria's Secret sprays, pieces of maths homework held together by cute dog-printed washi tape. I wonder if that's something you can read on my face—cheap, broken desire. So I wear these dead eyes every day, because it's like wearing a black shirt—easy and looks just fine. I need these dead eyes, especially when the kinds of faces I really want to make are better made in the dark, against somebody else's neck. This conclusion to myself, the explanation for my scattered attention, it's kind of funny. Since when did I want to be fucked so badly?

I end up outside the flat of a guy I know. He's so excited about the one-night stand, the nothing more. And me? I'm excited about not going home, about imagining very briefly that I'm normal. I sit on the stairs outside with my head tilted against my bag, wondering if it will turn him on to find me looking lost and tired like this.

I suddenly imagine something strange: I'm sat in a dark room with a swarm of butterflies walking along my skin. The butterflies he gives me, they aren't on the inside, like the drop in your gut on a rollercoaster—it's not like that, it's different. It's all on the outside, they're walking on the outside of my skin. I can't quite explain.

I check the time and it's only been two minutes, but that image of me, with the swarm of butterflies walking along my skin, it's starting to hurt somehow. There is a heat building in my cheeks and chest from the butterflies, which are now growing teeth, so I walk up and down his street to cool off. I've walked so far that I'm getting winded. Putting my hands on my knees I try to breathe. Where is he anyway? I text him, but no response. *Why am I here?* I ask myself and it's a stupid, stupid answer: I want him to want me so much that I don't have to want myself. He responds, 'Where are you?'

I'm not the kind of person you can ask that question to. He's inviting a woman with all of this jagged writing scratched across her body into his bed. He'll never understand the loose, looped handwriting across the chest he wants to put in his mouth.

I walk forwards, the streetlights like spotlights to the swarm of butterflies. Under that harsh light, I swallow hard and see they were never butterflies, just flies. And he's one of them. So I drag myself home instead, watching the neon store signs glowing at 2 AM and a little rain starting against tilted roofs.

While my hand is shaking around my bag for my keys, I see the Parrot again in her usual seat, staring down at me. At first I feel her judgment at my dishevelled self, but then there is a kindness in her beady eyes, one that my face against a pillow wasn't going to get me. She just looks at me, like I'm important, even with the whole street surrounding, she seems to choose me. I head inside and burn under the hot shower. The world is so beautiful outside; it makes me wonder what I've done to myself on the inside. Dead butterflies circle down the drain.

SHOULDN'T HAVE ASKED

I wish the world was this friendship. Our slapped foreheads, our gut-punched laughs.

'What happened to your hand?' she asks noticing the plaster, and I just mumble and shrug, not wanting to relive my Lidl fall. We joke about how we're eating ramen at a restaurant when that's all we eat in our flats too. 'Premium stuff,' I say, licking my lips and opening a can of ginger beer. The fizz in my ear taps against a few of my thoughts, so I make a mistake. I ask a question I know I shouldn't. Halfway to myself, a quarter-way to the crowd and the remainder to my friend, 'Why don't people like me?'

My face sours and I don't look up, because I'm listening and waiting to hear a response. But she doesn't say anything. She definitely heard me, but she can't say anything; instead she adjusts her glasses and searches her head. I'm looking up at her, my eyes heavy and hoping. She just mumbles and shrugs her shoulders. Afterwards, she looks at me, almost apologising because she's hurt watching me with my heavy, hoping eyes, knowing she can't tell me the answer. I have to hear myself say the reason why. I know that. I just haven't learned all of my lines yet. They are highlighted in yellow, and notes are made on the side. I just don't know them off by heart.

We say goodbye, and she hugs me extra tight.

A DARK DISASTER

I'm walking back home through Nicolson Street and I read that same graffiti again, *Where the lost things go, they grow.*

Is that a lyric from a song? A socialist slogan? I don't know. I'm trying to think about what it means when I'm knocked into by a group of drunk boys. They have the standard middle-parted English-boy hair, and those outfits like they're in *Dead Poets Society* at the age of twenty. I think they barely register me and keep walking, until I can feel one of them is looking at me and whispering. Even drunk, he's too polite to scream anything out. Their violence is always so passive, still sinister, but passive. I'm pretty sure that he won't do anything beyond this, so I forget it by the time I reach Princes Street.

I do that thing where I'm convinced I've lost my phone even though I just used it, so I get myself under a street-light and frantically check through my bag. Across the street from me is another girl; she's Indian too, with these silver jhumkas and long, silky hair. I want to talk to her, to tell her something that maybe only she could understand, but I don't really know what it is. Maybe it's just an impulse to talk in the silence of the dark.

I still rustle around my bag for my phone, relieved when I find it and check the time: 00:49. When I look up, I see those drunk English boys, six of them. They have no expression on their faces; they are just walking up behind the girl. It doesn't take a second for me to catch her eyes and dart back and forth between her and the boys. I am convinced they might do something to her, but she barely registers me and walks past them, gripping the hand of a man who must be her partner. It strikes me now just how wrong perceptions can be. I didn't even realise there was someone standing next to her. Maybe I'm just constantly trying to turn anything similar to me into me. And those boys are on the most popular street in Edinburgh. I'm just paranoid.

I think back to the graffiti to distract me, *Where the lost things go, they grow.* I start googling it while I'm walking. *A song from* Mary Poppins—*no, I don't think that's it. Oh right, I forgot Emily Blunt played her, I haven't watched that version, maybe I should.* I'm thinking these things while I feel that I am being followed. It's them again, but I'm trying to ignore that thought. It's a coincidence. I tell myself I'll stick to walking under streetlights, just to be safe—at least I'll be visible then. No, that's not good enough. I'll take one of the night buses.

I'm waiting at the bus stop, checking my phone and hoping they'll keep walking past me, but they stop where I am. If they're going to be on the same bus, I may as well just walk it. I start up again, and my heart sinks, drowning in my gut, when they start following me again. I don't know what to do with this.

The phantom feelings are walking in reality now. They are behind me, breathing down my neck, grabbing my bag to hold me still. A beige Wall Street coat is standing in front of me. I don't dare to look up. The streetlight starts to flicker above us, and suddenly it's all in strobe.

He spits when he talks to his friends, 'She's ugly, leave it.' There's roaring laughter behind me, but I'm just waiting for it to pass. I haven't tried to run yet, but this kicks me into consciousness, so I try relentlessly to get past the beige coat. He keeps sidestepping and chanting something to his Dead Poets Boys, which I don't register until he shoves me to the ground.

'Oi, come on. Let's go now,' one of them says, stepping over me, while the beige coat stares at me intently, punching me with his slow blinking, kicking me with his lashes. The rest of them are walking away, but he keeps staring at me, as if he has to finish this off. He can't leave until he's satisfied. So, he bends down, adjusting his trousers before he does, and pinches my face in his ring-wearing hand.

'It's just disgusting. I'm not trying to have a moan at you, but come on. Look at you.' His face is cringing while he gently removes my blue butterfly pin from my hair, laughing while he looks at it and then at me, like it doesn't make sense. 'It's just so fucking disgusting.' I want to ask him, what is? Which part is disgusting? But I can't move. I know I can't move. I know I can't say one word. So I just look down, but this annoys him. He slaps me. Once he's done it the first time, he decides he likes it, because passive was always going to be aggressive. He does it again. Then again. And again. Stinging and shaking my face. When he's finally finished, he becomes a blur starting to walk away.

I stay still under the flickering streetlight, playing Blanche DuBois, relying on the kindness of strangers. It's just strangers aren't kind to my kind. I'm left, a disaster in the dark.

I'm trying to get up. I'm really trying to get up. I want to cry but I can only do one thing at a time, and right now, I'm trying to get up. I put everything I have into pushing off of my hands and knees, but I still can't do it. I try again, digging into the ground with my palms and trying to build momentum, but my palms skid and I hit my head against the ground. 'Fuck,' I shout into my chest, gripping onto my shirt and spitting while I start to cry uneasy tears. I'm trying to fight them, but I have something to say, and the struggling tears come with the words, 'This is where you want me? Fine. Then fine.'

While I'm blurring my vision and mumbling words in my choking voice, I hear something that makes everything stop. I immediately scramble up into a sitting position, wiping my eyes and quietening my voice. There it is again. Over the Balmoral I see what's making that noise. The bone-jumping squawk is coming from the Parrot. Again, with a force like no other, she squawks, her screech ripping holes into any sound I have ever known, burning rails down any thought I have ever had.

She is flying at an extraordinary speed, her wings blue-frosted arrows, slicing through the air, head like a bullet, the pink flower a weapon in her mouth. Again, she squawks. That sound is thunder in my slapped skin. Her speed shows no sign of slowing down as she flies lower and lower, till she's the same level as my head. The Parrot stops suddenly in front of my face and I'm stunned to hear that in her screech are words: 'When reality rips you apart, you need to find something to tear it back with. Then you can see how you both fit together.'

Before I can take her words in, I see the beige coat is still visible in the distance, and so does the Parrot. Her wings slice across my face as she shoots past me, chasing the beige coat, who does not know she is coming. She lands on his head violently, ripping at his hair and squawking her mighty squawk against his face. I'm afraid of how far she'll go, watching her wings turning in an orange–blue–green cycle around him. Lucky for him his friends come to his aid, shooing her away before any real damage is done. But there is still fear lingering in my gut.

I lift my limp legs and find energy to stand. I can't see the Parrot anymore though I constantly look backwards and forwards for her. She is completely lost in the dark distance. But I hear her mighty squawk, the break of dawn in electric-blue darkness.

In the snap of a second, in a stroke of lightning, I see the Parrot is there again, as if she cuts under the folds of space and time. She is flying right towards me, with a laser-like focus I have never seen before. It's almost attacking, the look in her eyes, and when she squawks again it bleeds my mind. I begin to run, in some ways away from her and in some ways in imitation of her speedy flight.

The Parrot lands against my back, sending flashing pain through my body, as if biting through every single nerve. I scream. My voice cracks and howls, uneven and untuned, wild in its whimpers, spitting sparks flying from my mouth. Loud and mighty, there are jagged bright lines of violence in my voice, fireworks shooting between scorching flames. My hands race around to get her off, but I eventually stop feeling the turning of her feathers and webbed feet. Crazy, I'm turning around myself in circles, but she is gone. Frantic, I put my hands under my shirt and feel around my back in case she is there. There is something. Fresh, a tattoo—the wings of a Parrot bleeding into my back.

I stand alone, the air whipping my shirt up so that the wind's healing hands are held cool against my burning tattoo. In the briefly empty street, I make a silly face and imitate the mighty squawk of a Parrot—the sound crashing thoughts, sifting images, freeing feelings. All questions are divided into screeching answers.

LIGHTNING BIRD

Let me listen to my own voice
For once
In this endless noise

Moving mouth
Becomes personal maze

A Barbie girl in Legoland
A different plastic, in a different shade

And on my tongue
There is a taste
like a lightning bird—
a sonic storm that I made

And so I say

Let me listen to my own voice
For once
In this endless noise

OCTOBER FOR ANOTHER CENTURY

Nur Turkmani

Song: Bedouin Burger, Zeid Hamdan *et* Lynn Adib – 'Ya Man Hawa'

I haven't looked in the mirror in months.
My shame is a rock by the sea,
I kick it because it won't budge.
The days rain like a dried-up river,
even our skies are contaminated,
and I keep thinking of this poet's line:
Where do birds fly after the last sky?
Since the earthquakes
I can't stop looking at chandeliers.
I hide from the day and its river.
I hide from memory like a fault line.
What do you trust if the ground, too, betrays?
This photographer tells me
he no longer believes in what he does. *I want to shoot a gun.*
This dancer tells me she began colouring
during the war. *It's because there isn't a point.*
Enough with the sun, she says.
October shouldn't be allowed
to break.
Look, if good art asks us to make room for grey—
something's wrong. Something's very wrong.
I no longer want to create.
Teach me to destroy.

THE DAMAGE HAS BEEN DONE

Mandy Shunnarah

Song: MASTER BOOT RECORD – 'BIOS'

'Yesterday the Israeli Prime Minister's office said that it had confirmed Hamas beheaded babies & children while we were live on the air. The Israeli government now says today it CANNOT confirm babies were beheaded. I needed to be more careful with my words and I am sorry.'
— tweet by CNN reporter Sara Sidner, 12 October 2023

If only apologies could bring the dead back—
uncrush the child's skull under stories of fallen
apartment buildings, unspool the bullet from
the pregnant woman's back, unairstrike Gaza.

If only newspaper corrections issued hours
or days later—& always at the bottom of the page
—could resurrect our martyrs. Restore
the child's skin so parents could identify his face.

If only propaganda were an innocent mistake
that didn't lead to a boy stabbed in Chicago
& calls for Palestinians to be hunted in Dearborn.
O 'innocent mistake,' that fatal oxymoron.

If only regretful notes could be printed on shrouds,
then those apologies would be good for something.
The damage has been done. Our morgues are full,
as well as our ice cream trucks, & our mass graves.

We're running out of flags & white sheets to bury
our dead. Sorry doesn't even begin to cover it.

MITES

Aurora Leode Fadonougbo

Song: Abdullah Ibrahim – 'Mindiff'

We were full of rage.

So much rage that the moment he left what was supposed to be our love nest *forever*, we immediately occupied his empty shelves, without honouring or mourning his absence.

Our story ended like that, on a hot and utterly trivial Thursday at the end of August, when we still had big plans for autumn and he kept promising us things would change.

And yes, they did change.

We vividly remember the feeling of relief as we sat on the couch in a half-empty home, finding ourselves truly alone for the first time. In those new silences, which still haunt us from time to time, we would have loved to cry and feel lost without him, but we never managed to do it.

Our love had been a great love, and we had imagined the end of a great love as slippery, full of tears and loneliness, not angry and dry.

In the days following the breakup, our eyes remained red and sticky, just as they had been for months, and showed no signs of healing. Like all the major health upheavals we had faced over the years, that annoying conjunctivitis seemed like a clear warning, an inevitable curse. Before discovering our rage, in fact, we were convinced that the redness of our eyes was telling us, *You'll cry, oh, how you'll cry!*

But when he actually left, we didn't cry at all. On the contrary, we jealously kept all the tears stagnant in the back of our eyes. We rediscovered ourselves as determined, almost unhinged, as if we had embodied the image of the ravenous animal that our red eyes conferred upon us. We had a new role, and we chose to play it well, making that anger our sole belief.

When everything ended, we compared the vastness of the empty space he left behind in the house to the cramped one we all, despite being many, occupied. At night, we struggled to fall asleep and spent hours confusing memories and rewriting them again and again through that new red lens.

In the end, it even seemed that the entire story had only been something conjured by our irritated eyes—because it was they who filtered the past, who had fallen ill in the present, and who had been selectively blind when some of us had been forced into silence.

Our eyes, like tyrants imposing their sole vision over all the rest of our senses, became lost in the beauty of the graceful way his body moved. They had learned to read every subtle shift in his facial expression as a sign of changing desire. They had even glimpsed his potential future through the qualities they recognised as his greatest strengths. They watched how he smiled at those he loved, how his face lit up with passion, found comfort in observing how attentively he noticed the smallest details of the world, and ceased to be afraid when they saw the fire he radiated defending what he believed in.

They had managed to see all this and more in him with perfect clarity, stubbornly clinging to their ability to delve into his soul—without realising in time, however, that none of what they had discovered in him was ever meant for them, for whom he reserved only neglect.

During those sleepless nights, our rage expanded to the point of seeping out as a viscous, yellowish, sticky liquid from those idle eyeballs, hidden beneath soaked bandages.

We often thought about how much we wanted to erase the evidence of the past just to rid ourselves of that constant itch, because for us, one was inseparable from the other.

Yet love is one of the few things in life that, when it ends, carries with it the insidious doubt that it might never have been there from the beginning, and it constantly needs to leave tangible traces of its past existence in a present that is utterly foreign to it.

For us, who had so much rage, it felt like everything he had given us over the years had only ever been in response to what we had given first. We discovered we were loved through subtraction: for the bad things we weren't, for the negative things we didn't do, for the ugly things we didn't say... How our tear ducts burned when we thought about how he had never loved us through addition, for all the parts we were.

As we retraced the story of our ending, we analysed the painful marks of what now felt like a violent kind of love, because perhaps there's nothing more violent than not truly seeing another person in all their pieces.

We couldn't figure out which part of us he had exchanged loving glances with during our first meeting, and this tormented us.

Even though we were so many, in a short time he had managed to squeeze all of us into that narrow silhouette of the ideal woman he kept ready in the closet.

Maybe we were just passing by—nothing more than a coincidence—and he saw us, decided we'd fit perfectly in that cage, forced us inside, and crushed every part of us that didn't quite fit. As guilty as he was, for a long time we mistook those pushes for caresses, and now we were paying the price with our eyes, thirsty for true reciprocity.

When the itch became unbearable, we often convinced ourselves that we had become allergic to him, to his insecurities, to his unbearable crocodile tears, always too many compared to ours. In those moments, we were almost certain we had developed a physical intolerance to the way he appeared sad about our achievements or our happiness, or to his fear of how others perceived our body.

Yet now that he is gone, we're still treating this chronic conjunctivitis, which, we later discover, was an allergic reaction—not to him, but to mites. It's been a year since we last saw him and since those days we spent locked in the house, afraid of making things worse.

And even if we're still paying the price for that mutual emotional blindness, we've stopped existing solely to fulfil his need for love.

Maybe the tears we never cried could have helped us shed that dusty life-for-two more quickly and step outside, all together and without shame, into the sunlight, where mites die.

Now, thinking about mites—their invisible multitude, unseen by the naked eye, all lumped together under the word 'dust'—almost makes us smile.

Maybe what we believed was a warning was actually the verdict of a war we had already lost. *You will bleed, oh, how you will bleed!*

In the end, when our rage grew like mites—spreading into every corner, covering every surface, stubborn, layered, impossible to ignore—it was too late to clean up the mess.

LABOUR DAY, MAY 1

Nicole Morris

Song: Tiken Jah Fakoly – 'Plus rien ne m'étonne (Live Salle
Pleyel)'

if we light the fire at dusk with feet bare but hands
bound in pollen newly spent on this fresh spring
will it spark bright blue or smoulder down to a crimson bruise
smoke to coal to ash, a return to a thing unseen
soil then silt then moist then rot, then born again into seed
then sprout
this is the way it goes
with time and tides, the push pull rise fall of revolt, that sinking slop
of *what happened then* beside *it is happening now* on top of
but what of tomorrow

i'll tell you this

we have been here before in 2023, 1948, 1916, 1830, 1619, 1492
our bones keep score where our teeth have gone soft
and so, together we might thread our fingers in knots
so that an injury to one is an injury to all
and time the drop of our heel-toe stomp in measure with
hearts that have been stopped
by borders drawn in the ink of brutes and thieves
and in the light of day watch the smoke rise in prayer
to wipe us clean, the gift of razing the dark to receive the light of today
if we keep the fires lit, our blood might hold its heat
our throats might throw our screams in unison:
MAYDAY MAYDAY MAYDAY
enough

ATLANTA II
Banah el Ghadbanah

Song: Nxdia – 'OUCH'

& here are my hands they zip-tied blue
the blood constricted & in need of air,
& here my throat they choked without
remorse, & my back they bruised with
batons & here my dignity they tried to
defeat & here the blue lights they flood
my street with so that i never sleep &
here on my spine the strategies they
exchange like money between jerusalem
& atlanta, coughed up & spat onto my body
the one that is full of rolls for lovers & here
are my ears that never rest from the sound
of mosquito drones & here are my pupils
imprinted with the vision of my student
as they piled onto his frozen body & here
is my heart, shouting, 'follow me!'

THE FIREFLIES

Sarah F. Abdullahi

Song: Ed Sheeran – 'I See Fire'

Ilhan had spent her entire life trying to keep her brother calm. Now, again, his room pulsed with fury.

A shadow whispered past the kitchen window, waiting.

Her mother, fingers webbed with dough, craned to Ilhan with pleading eyes.

'Go, please, speak to him.'

Ilhan's heart thumped. She could hear them outside, sniffing by the front door.

She took the stairs in threes and didn't bother knocking before slipping into Mustafa's room. Her brother was still in his uniform, head balled into his chest, breathing deeply. Around him, the room was carnage.

'Hmm, lemme guess, farted in class again?' Ilhan broke the silence, her mouth dry and her pulse skittering.

'Go away,' Mustafa snapped.

She kept her voice light. 'It's okay, IBS is a natural experience. We will still accept you. Well... Hooyo might. Not sure about me. That's pretty embarrassing.'

Silence.

'At least they didn't give you a nickname.' Ilhan resisted biting her nails. Fear was fine, anything was fine, so long as it wasn't anger. 'I knew this one kid in school called Idris whose breath stank so bad that everyone called him Iblis.'

Silence. She inched closer and poked his side.

'Wanna know why? Cos every time he spoke, it felt like cathaab.'

81

That earned her a sharp exhale. She sank into the bed next to him, giving in to the impulse to bite her nails. There was almost nothing left of them, but she rubbed the edges of her chewed skin against her canines anyway as her brother unfurled. His eyes were bloodshot and the bottom of his face was contorted. She automatically moved to smooth his mouth but he batted away her hand with hard eyes.

'Leave me alone.'

'What's up?' The bed creaked lower as she shifted closer to him. The wind outside was quiet, but she kept one ear out for downstairs. Would her mother shout for her if they came inside? No, she told herself, she wouldn't let that happen. She had this under control.

But Mustafa's face was thunderous.

'Is it the teachers? Honestly, they are always the worst.' Her voice was soft, appeasing—it was easier to take the edge off this way. 'I had a teacher once—'

'It's never fair,' he spat. 'They never care about the truth. They think they know everything.'

Relief flooded through her. Just a teachers-pick-on-me rant.

'They're bullies,' she agreed. 'Sad weirdos. It is so much easier to ignore them than to let them bother you.'

'Ignore it? How can I ignore it? He was lying,' Mustafa erupted. 'He told the whole class that Hakim had been kicked out for bad behaviour. How can he lie like that? And no one except me and my friend Moses defended him, and then he gave us both detention. For an hour. For telling the truth! How are they allowed to do that?' He was seething, his eyes wild.

She had misjudged it. 'Yes, of course.'

Somehow she'd made everything worse. His anger was getting more complicated the older he got. She wasn't sure how long she'd be able to manage it. A migraine was forming in her temples, and she closed her eyes as she made soothing noises. Downstairs, she heard a muffled bang.

Blood thrummed in her ears. She tried to keep her voice level.

'Listen, you are right and they are wrong.' Appeasement had been a mistake; she tried reassurance.

'But why doesn't it matter if I'm right? They don't listen, they don't care.' His voice was thickening, a tell-tale sign.

She let the silence of the room kill the rest of his fury. Only when his breathing had evened, and she had stopped shivering, and whatever had creaked up the stairs had slinked back down, did she speak again.

'They win if you let them upset you...'

She rarely ever brought up the fireflies, which was what she called them, around Mustafa. For him, their presence was a source of antagonism. She needed him steady.

Years before their arrival, her Awoowo had once pointed at the few surviving stars in the light-polluted London sky and told her how those twinkling lights were actually burning balls. *We aren't the only ones that love to sit and watch fire.* She had glanced at the blackened husk of Grenfell Tower in the distance and wondered if something across the stars had mistaken its burning for starlight. She didn't have to wait long. The fireflies came soon after.

Ilhan had hoped that not knowing anything but a world carefully emptied of anger, her brother would be safe. But it had been the opposite. It had been five months since they'd stopped his anger therapy. Ilhan made a mental note to find more shifts for the money. He wasn't managing well anymore. Mustafa was twelve now, but he had been seething like this since he was six.

'He lied about Hakim,' he repeated.

His eyes were wet. Good, grief was good.

'Who was this?' Ilhan murmured.

'Mr Calpo, in History.'

'I'll write an email.' But now Mustafa was crying, hard. She wrapped an arm around him and he sank his face into her shoulder. He rarely sought comfort like this anymore.

'Don't you ever feel mad? Like really mad?' He looked up at her.

'Dunno. Don't have time for all of that, cos I have to take care of your smelly bum.'

'You never take anything seriously, Ilhan.' His voice dropped low, disappointed.

Ilhan smiled blandly. She couldn't begin to explain any of it to him, or to her parents. For some people to never get angry, some people had to stop being people, turn themselves into nothing, offer no obstacles. She had learnt to be so cold for them that sometimes she wondered if she had accidentally frozen herself.

Outside his door, she was reminded why. She saw how close they'd got. There was a deep scratch mark on the wooden banister at the top of the stairs. She flung a towel over it and hurried down. Keeping Mustafa away from his anger was the only thing that mattered. It exhausted her.

The living room window had been prised wide open, and Ilhan closed it with trembling fingers.

When she opened the kitchen door, acrid smoke hung in the air. Her mother was humming. She turned and smiled at Ilhan with a forced brightness that didn't match her eyes.

'He's fine,' Ilhan offered.

Hooyo rolled her eyes. 'Of course,' she huffed, 'boys!' and turned back to flip the blackened sabaayad smouldering on her pan.

Mustafa stayed steady for three more weeks. Except for a near miss returning with shopping as they passed a screaming homeless man opposite Bush Green. Mustafa had tugged off his VR link, his eyes deglazing quickly.

'What are they doing?' he whispered, stiffening next to Ilhan.

The fireflies had also turned towards the screams and were closing in a semi-circle around the homeless man, who winked in and out between their long bodies and machete claws.

'Put it back on,' Ilhan insisted.

But he left it off, looking keenly around. 'Why is no one doing anything? Why are we letting this happen to him?' His voice tightened as he turned hard eyes on the people shuffling around them.

A sole firefly twitched and sniffed the air. It turned bulbous eyes on them and took sharp steps forward, but Ilhan was already dragging her brother down the street. By the time they hit Uxbridge Road, her chest burned and lights were dancing in her eyes. Mustafa spat on the floor and cursed but glanced back in fear.

When they arrived home, he refused to acknowledge her for the rest of the week. He finally broke this punishment when she came by his room with a pack of Marylands and a haughty expression.

He snivelled and begged her, and Ilhan grinned and split open the packet. In between bites, she casually suggested it was time to restart therapy, and he nodded, cookie dust sprinkled around his mouth.

When Mustafa finally exploded, two months later, it was at school. He had got so angry over something, they said, that no one could calm him as he stood half crying, half shouting about an injustice. A firefly had been lingering around the school and caught the warmth of his rage. It had descended like a plunging bird. When the headteacher returned, it was still chewing. By the time their mother arrived, there was nothing left of him but a pile of gleaming bones. The head handed the box to Hooyo with a solemn smile. 'We tried to help him, truly. We did our best.'

When a loved one dies, it is an unfathomable thing. Over the box of his polished remains, they watched the door and waited for Mustafa to come home. Steaming food sat on the floor. A fresh mango lassi sweated. The box would block his view to the television, but Mustafa would move it when he got here. Hooyo sat upright. Aabo was slumped. Ilhan hovered somewhere in the middle.

Eventually the food cooled and the drink separated, and Aabo began to spoon bariis into his mouth. Hooyo shot him a strained smile, but he ignored her. He stood a few minutes later, pausing briefly as his eyes landed on the bones, then shook his head in disbelief and left for his shift.

Only then did Ilhan feel it. A warm ember like a struck match in her chest. She blinked, her breath hitching at the heat. It flickered in her throat and made something in her stomach burn. She raced up the stairs, unplugged her headset and slid it on. Immediately, lights and noise flashed endlessly across her field of vision. She pulled up TikTok and watched a stream of videos until the ember was a coal again.

When she trailed back downstairs, her limbs were heavy.

Then she saw the box again, and the fire burst like it had only been waiting, not fully quenched. Ilhan felt all of her searing, red-hot anger. It burst the world into furious definition, into unbearable colour. For the first time, she could see everything clearly. In the living room: the orange glow of the lamplight; the iron burn on the side of the couch; how the small, thin box should not have been able to contain her little brother. In this bursting world, she could see the thin rage under her mother's countenance like translucent, spidery veins. She saw it pulse now in Hooyo's seething smile.

She understood why Mustafa hadn't been able to exist in black and white. After a lifetime of no colour, the saturation she'd hidden from herself was almost too blinding. But it felt good to feel.

Except the fire needed to go somewhere. Heart thrumming, Ilhan grabbed the box. She dragged it outside. It was heavier than she expected. Up close, it smelled like rotting flesh.

Rage rolled off her in hot waves. She placed the box in the middle of the road. Quickly, she attracted fireflies. They danced towards her with their long-limbed ghoulish bodies and bulging eyes, sniffing the air and gnashing their sharp, glittering mouths.

As she stared down at Mustafa's bones, a scream erupted out of her. It started as a low keening until it became a raging bellow. Curtains were drawn back. The estate became a sea of small square lights as people came to their windows to watch her tiny figure.

Ilhan lit a match and dropped it into the box. She took a few steps back. Every new thought caused a fresh wave of molten fury to prickle her skin and wet her face. Her uncorked rage was so potent that it was drawing hundreds of fireflies, all eager to consume her heat. The residential street was quickly filled. The fireflies drew in so close that she could hear their quick, anticipating breath like low laughter.

'Ilhan!'

Hooyo was sobbing by the estate door. Ilhan stared blindly at her for a second. Then, somehow, she found a way to hold the heat and switched it off. The anger, rage and fury—she swallowed it all down like a lump and hid its light. Her world turned black and white again.

The fireflies froze in confusion like scattered street-lamps, but their hunger carried them forward, and, starved of anger, they took the fire for second best. Ilhan watched as they raced past her, one by one, into the flames, and when they burned, finally, so did she.

THE BLACKSMITH II

Gospel Chinedu

Song: Chase Noseworthy – 'Blacksmith, Blacksmith'

The intention was to ignite the lion in my body. That strong will to end each day undead. So, he cast me into the forge, black & steel, & watched me become yellow with fear. He said, the fiercest fire of a fighter is his desire. & rage & fear are just adrenaline gushing out like running water. He stood by & watched me seethe, like his father watched him. Then, he pulled me out of the forge & placed my body on the anvil. Same way Christ was laid on the crucifix, holy, yet guilty with the offences of the world. 1 was malleable & prepared to be hammered into whatever shape my father wanted me in. He wanted me in the shape of a 'Y'—double-winged with a quick spine bevelled with grace. He was carved in the shape of an 'O'—a hole where his father, who was carved in the shape of an 'i' with a dot too heavy with the sorrow of war & slavery, emptied his sorrows. Then, he picked me with the tong & cast my 'Y'-shaped body into the forge, again, until my yellow fear became a red desire. He pulled me out, again. & cast me in again. & again. & again. & then, he finally pulled me out. & dipped me into the pool of his eyes to harden the steel of my desire. He said, *be ready to fight for your life.* & to be ready to fight is to be ready to die. So he made me a fine hilt & hid me in a scabbard. & because he wanted me to always be prepared, every day, he would lay me on the anvil & hone the edges of my desire with his father's whetstone.

A COUNTRY THAT CARRIES ITS DEAD LIKE FIREWOOD

Oladosu Michael Emerald

Song: Burna Boy feat. Chris Martin – 'Monsters You Made'

Once, my father told me the heart
of a nation is a well. Pour too much
grief into it, & the rope breaks. I have
watched my country bend under the weight
of loss, its people gathering pieces of
themselves from the rubble of history.
In the north, Deborah's body is a bonfire.
We do not pray to the ashes anymore;
we scatter them into the harmattan & wait.
Lekki was a river of red. October carries
the memory like a scar, its edges raw,
its centre a question no one answers.
Justice sits in a courtroom, its hands tied,
its mouth gagged, its eyes turned to the past.
But listen—even silence has a pulse; even despair
speaks of what can be built again. The sky is heavy
with names, but it is also heavy with rain. Something
is coming—you can feel it in the air. If unity is a song,
then let it be loud enough to drown the sound of bullets.
Let it be a hand extended, pulling us from the brink into
the light of ourselves.

ABOUT THE AUTHORS

Sarah F. Abdullahi is a speculative fiction writer based in London who enjoys writing about time, madness, and aliens. She has a bachelor's in English and Creative Writing and is an alumna of City Lit and a member of Brixton Writers Circle. She is currently working on her first novel.

Yasmin Alrabiei is an Iraqi writer and researcher based in London. With academic roots in Neuroscience and Cognitive Science, her work explores the intersection of scientific inquiry and spirituality, challenging the contemporary, academic, and often Western compulsion to divide the two. She is particularly drawn to the psychological imprints of cultural memory and the neural architecture of nostalgia. Her writing has appeared in *Kahf Magazine*, *Mille World*, *ICON Magazine*, and *Dazed MENA*.

Mymona Bibi is a Bengali-British writer, creative facilitator, and ESOL teacher based in Newcastle upon Tyne. She is interested in themes of cities, multilingualism, inequality, and home. Her writing has been featured in the Ilkley Literature Festival, *Magma Poetry*, *Butcher's Dog*, and Lumpen Press. She has produced and performed at events such as the Newcastle Fringe Festival (2023 and 2025) and NOVUM (2023 and 2024). Currently, she is the lead artist of the World Writes multilingual community writing group. You can find her on Instagram @wordsbymymona.

Gospel Chinedu is a Nigerian poet of Igbo descent. He is currently an undergraduate student at the College of Health

Sciences, Okofia, where he studies Anatomy. He loves music and is a big fan of Isak Danielson. His poems are mostly speculative and cut across different themes. He is a 2021 Starlit Award Winner; 1st Runner Up for the 2023 Blurred Genre Contest (Invisible City Lit); recipient of an Honourable Mention in the 2023 Stephen A. DiBiase Poetry Prize; and a finalist in the 2023 Dan Veach Prize for Younger Poets. His works of poetry have appeared or are forthcoming in *Chestnut Review, Worcester Review, Augur Magazine, Fantasy, FIYAH, The Deadlands, Channel, Apparition Lit, Mud Season Review, Trampset, The Drift, Consequence Forum, The Rialto, BathMagg*, and other places. Gospel tweets @gonspoetry.

Aria Danaparamita (Mita) is a queer migrant artist, writer, and organiser engaged in decolonial justice. Their work traverses poetry, prose, photography, and film, and explores the intersections of art, archive, and abolition. Born in Indonesia and currently living in the UK, they are deeply informed in their practice by their revolutionary heritage and grassroots organising with communities resisting coloniality and oppression. They received their bachelor's degree from Wesleyan University (USA) and a master's degree from SOAS University of London (UK).

Oladosu Michael Emerald (he/him) is a writer, artist, and actor. He is the author of *Every Little Thing That Moves*, an art editor at *Surging Tide* magazine, editor at *MAAR Review*, and an instructor at The Arnheim Art Gallery, Young Artists Art Hub, and The Anasa Collection. He is the winner of the Off the Limit Art Contest (2024), Sprinng Poetry Contest (2024), Garden Party Collective Neurodivergent Poetry Contest (2025), and *Sine Qua Non* Inaugural Poetry Prize (2025). He has been published or is forthcoming in *Chestnut Review, FIYAH, Lolwe, Temz Review*, and elsewhere. He is the Pioneer Fellow of the Muktar Aliyu Art Residency. You can find him on X @garricologist, Instagram @garrycologist, and Facebook as Michael Emerald.

Aurora Leode Fadonougbo is an Afro-Italian writer born and raised in Milan. She writes in Italian, working across narrative, poetry, and critical essays. Holding a master's degree in Oriental and African Studies, she draws from geographic and imaginative landscapes deeply rooted in Italian, Beninese, and Japanese cultural heritage. Her work, fuelled by a profound fascination with the human soul, seeks to celebrate beauty, reclaim narratives, and take a political stance in the world. 'Mites' is her first published work—a lyrical exploration in magical realism, where the real and the surreal intertwine to reveal emotional and symbolic truths.

Banah el Ghadbanah's last name literally means angry in Arabic (they just feminised their given name, because who needs more male rage in the world?). They are the author of the poetry book *La Syrena: Visions of a Syrian Mermaid from Space* (Dzanc Books), which won the Diverse Voices Prize in 2022. You can find their work in *What's Afghan Punk Rock, Anyway?*, *Mizna*, *The Women's Review of Books*, and more. They hold a PhD in Ethnic Studies and research Syrian women's creativity in revolution and war.

Nafeesa H. (born in Kashmir in 1993, bred in Birmingham) is a poet, playwright, educator, performer, and director. When she's not archiving city council bankruptcy, Nafeesa uses an inter-sectional approach to her multi-disciplinary creative practice. Her poetry collection *Besharam* (Verve Poetry Press) was highly commended in the 2019 Forward Prizes. Nafeesa is published in the Forward anthology *Poems of the Decade 2011–2020*, among other publications, and has appeared on BBC Bitesize, BBC Radio 4 Comedy, and *The Verb*, and at international literary festivals. She is currently a scholarship MA Writing Poetry student at Poetry School London, continuing to develop a body of work about corner shop culture, car boots, faith, and divine love.

Malak Hijazi is a Palestinian writer from Gaza. Her work explores memory, grief, and place under occupation and genocide. She writes non-fiction and poetry, with pieces published in *The Electronic Intifada, Mizna, Pleiades Magazine*, We Are Not Numbers, and others. She holds an MA in Comparative Literature, focusing on spatial studies and the erasure of place in Palestinian literature.

Malika McKenney is a writer and artist from Miami, Florida. Her work explores place, belonging, and our relationship to the natural world. She is the co-winner of the Grierson Verse Prize (2025) and a recent graduate from the University of Edinburgh in English Literature and History.

Simran Kaur Johal writes in spaces lingering between memory, language, and the weight of being seen. She writes with the intention of an intuitive grasp of the personal as political, outlining reflections on resistance, identity, and the quiet forces that shape our lives. Outside of her prose and poetry, she writes reviews on literature, music, and film, with a recent interest in the life and work of Labi Siffre.

Jiaqi Kang is a writer and the founding editor-in-chief of *Sine Theta Magazine*, an international, print-based creative arts publication by and for the Sino diaspora. They are the winner of the 2022 *White Review* Short Story Prize and a recipient of fellowships from Lambda Literary and the Fine Arts Work Center. Originally from Geneva, Switzerland, they are currently based in England. Jiaqi knows that Palestine will be free in our lifetimes, from the river to the sea.

Laetitia Keok is a writer and editor based between New York City and Singapore. Her work has been placed for the Adrienne Rich Award for Poetry and the Oxford Poetry Prize, supported by the Fine Arts Work Center in Provincetown and the National Arts Council of Singapore, and published in *Poetry Northwest*, *Split Lip Magazine*, and *Wildness*, amongst others. Laetitia holds an MFA in Poetry from New York University, and edits for *Gaudy Boy* and *Sine Theta Magazine*.

Bidhya Limbu is a Nepali-Singaporean writer and early-career bereavement care researcher living in London. Her work has been published or is forthcoming in *Midway Journal*, *Atelier of Healing*, and elsewhere. She has received support from the *Kenyon Review* Writers Workshop. She is a student of grief.

Nicole Morris is a working-class, biracial Black girl poet who writes essays. Her work contends with the intersections of identity, grief, and coloniality through the lens of motherhood. She has been featured in North American and Irish journals such as *The Stinging Fly*, *Banshee*, *The Indiana Review*, Roxane Gay's *The Audacity*, and elsewhere. Nicole's writing has been supported by Tin House, DISQUIET, and Roots.Wounds. Words. Originally from Los Angeles, she lives near the sea in Western Ireland.

Rasheed Rollins is a writer of Afro-Caribbean heritage from south-east London. His writing was shortlisted in Penguin's WriteNow 2020 programme. He is working on his debut novel, which explores the community, devastation, and past orbiting two former lovers during a summer in London.

Mandy Shunnarah (they/them) is an Alabama-born Appalachian and Palestinian-American writer in Columbus, Ohio. Their essays, poetry, and short stories have been published in *The New York Times*, *Electric Literature*, *The Rumpus*, and others. Their first book, *Midwest Shreds: Skating Through America's Heartland*, was released in 2024 from Belt

Publishing, and their second book, a poetry collection titled *We Had Mansions*, was published by Diode Editions in 2025. Read more at mandyshunnarah.com.

Nur Turkmani is a researcher and writer from Beirut. She studied Creative Writing at the University of Oxford and Politics at the London School of Economics and the American University of Beirut. Her research explores agriculture, social movements, and displacement. Her fiction and poetry have appeared in *The Missouri Review, New England Review, Copper Nickel, The Rumpus, Poetry London, Columbia Journal, The Adroit Journal*, and elsewhere. Her essays have been published in *Evergreen Review, Al-Jumhuriya, Jadaliyya*, and *Rusted Radishes*. *October*, her debut poetry collection, is forthcoming from Hajar Press.

Christian Yeo Xuan (he/they) is a poet, novelist, playwright, and actor based in Singapore by way of Beirut and Paris. His work has been published or is forthcoming in *Oxford Poetry, Indiana Review, The Mays*, and *New Singapore Poetries*, among others. He has placed or been a finalist for the *Washington Square Review* New Voices Award, the National Poetry Competition, the *Poetry London* Pamphlet Prize, and the Bridport Prize. He has received support from the *Kenyon Review* Writers Workshop, Tin House, and the National Arts Council. His website is christianyeoxuan.com.

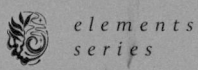

elements
series

The Hajar Book of Rage ignites the first spark in the *elements* anthology series, harnessing the primordial force of fire as a fury that destroys and transforms. Bringing together fiction, poetry and essays by writers of colour, this Fire-themed collection delves into the fierce, animating power of rage as a catalyst for revolutionary change.

Here, rage teaches. It reveals what we're fighting against and what we're fighting for. It mobilises us into action, rouses our ideals and refuses to let us compromise. And it is unruly and consuming—a blaze that resists containment.

This is a searing tribute to the fires of anger that fuel our resistance and burn down the worlds that cannot hold us.

Sarah F. Abdullahi
Yasmin Alrabiei
Mymona Bibi
Gospel Chinedu
Aria Danaparamita
Oladosu Michael Emerald
Aurora Leode Fadonougbo
Banah el Ghadbanah
Nafeesa H.
Malak Hijazi

Simran Kaur Johal
Jiaqi Kang
Laetitia Keok
Bidhya Limbu
Malika McKenney
Nicole Morris
Rasheed Rollins
Mandy Shunnarah
Nur Turkmani
Christian Yeo Xuan

www.hajarpress.com

ISBN 978-1-914221-34-7

Hajar
Press

9 781914 221347 >

FSC®